The Window

Boe Healy & Chisto Healy

BAYNAM BOOKS PRESS

Book Cover by Christy Aldridge

Illustrations by Crystal Baynam

Editor Chisto Healy

For Mommy

CONTENTS

PROLOGUE
WHERE IT BEGAN

Ghostly Halloween Superstore October 2011

Cody Wilson came bursting through the front doors of the crowded store, panting and panicked. Blood spattered his face and clothes. "Call the police!" he screamed. "Please. He's following me!"

People were all staring and murmuring now. An animatronic of the Death Digger went off and slashed with his scythe. Cody jumped and yelped, which only made people murmur more. They were looking and talking about him like he was behind the glass at the zoo. He started to cry. "You have to call the police! If he gets here, he's going to kill us all."

A beautiful black girl with purple hair and a nose ring, wearing a Candyman T-shirt, working behind the counter, took out her golden phone, which was covered in glitter. She dialed quietly and held it to her ear as she continued to watch Cody nervously. He kept looking over his shoulder at the front door like he expected it to fly open at any second, allowing an axe-wielding maniac to enter.

The manager of the store came over to him. He was wearing a Ghostface shirt behind suspenders whose straps were covered in pins from various horror films. "Who?" he asked. "Who are you afraid of? What's happened?"

Cody remembered in flashes. The gunshots. Blood. Screams. Running. "The Windows," he said. "He's using the windows."

"Who?"

"Truman Woodking at the old house in the forest."

The manager looked confused. "He stays to himself. What were you doing out there? Hey, I know you. You're Cody Wilson, Jamie's brother."

At those words, Cody shuddered. Memories came crashing into his mind. *"I think he's gone," Jamie said with a sly grin. "Let's go in."*

"I don't know," Cody said. "What if he's dangerous?"

"He's just one old weirdo living in the woods. I'm on the track team, little bro. We'll just leave him in the dust."

"But I'm not on the track team. If he lives out here, he probably hunts. What if he's got a gun or dogs?"

"Do you see any dogs?" Kyle Burns asked with a chuckle and a shake of his bangs that only covered one eye in yellow hair.

"Doesn't mean there aren't any," Cody told him, looking warily at the big dilapidated black house. "Who paints their house black?"

"I bet you can't even see it at night," said Tamara, Kyle's girlfriend, tracing her finger around the inner circle of her hoop earring. "What if there's bodies in there?" She laughed.

Cody didn't see the humor. "What if there are? Shouldn't we not be there so we don't join them?"

A supportive hand came down on his shoulder, and he looked up into the calming blue eyes of Cole, Jamie's boyfriend. "I understand why you're scared," Cole said. "Your points are valid. You're rational. We need someone like you, but we're not going to do anything crazy, I promise. It's just a little Halloween time fun. We always explore abandoned houses."

"It's not abandoned," Cody told him quietly.

"I know. Truman lives here, but he's not here now, and he lives alone, so it's close enough. If we run into any trouble, we'll leave right away, I promise. I'll keep you safe." Cody looked over at his brother, who gave him a reassuring smile and nodded. Cody sighed with reluctance but smiled back and gave a nod of his own.

The vision fast-forwarded. There was a bang. Tamara was screaming. Kyle was on his back in the leaves around the side of the tall black wooden house. Cody was frozen, staring. Kyle was missing his eye, and the leaves were turning red around his head, it was flowing outward like a pestilence, changing all the leaves it touched and racing toward his Spiderman shoes.

"Where did it come from?" Jamie was yelling. He was looking at the house but saw nothing.

"You said we'd go. We have to go," Cody was saying, but his voice was so quiet, he couldn't even hear it himself.

Jamie and Cole were holding Kyle's wrists and dragging him through the leaves, spreading the red further through the yellow and orange leaves of Autumn that rained down about them, a woodland shower of citrus.

"Was it a gun?" Cole asked, looking back toward the house.

"I don't know. I don't know," Jamie said through tears. Tamara was stumbling behind them like she had drunk a lot of beer.

Cody hadn't moved yet. He couldn't. His legs forgot how to work. He saw a shadow behind the window, a flash of movement. "He's at the window," he said, but there was no one to hear it.

He looked back at his brother and his friends, hoping he could say it louder this time, but before he could say anything, his brother's head exploded. He saw it before he heard it. It didn't seem real. His brother was looking right at him, staring into his eyes, and then his face was gone, and blood was everywhere. There was a thunderclap, and then Jamie was on the ground.

"Jamie?" he asked, little more than a whisper. Cole had let go of Kyle's limp arm and was running back for him. "It's the windows," Cody mumbled. "He's using the windows."

"Get down!" Cole was screaming. "Stay low!" He was waving his arms. Tamara didn't follow him. Cody watched as she ran for the treeline. He didn't blame her. He knew he should be running, too. He just couldn't remember how. A glance back at the strangely leaning jet black house showed him a shadow passing by another window. Then he saw Truman. He was at an open window on the first floor. There was something in his hand.

Cody looked back at Tamara. She was almost free, almost safe, but a sound of whistling air found his ears, and then Tamara was attached to a tree, an arrow protruding from her back. She was still squirming and trying to get free. He would never forget the sound of her sobs and wails. Another arrow followed, and another, pinning her arms so she was hugging the tree against her will. She screamed and screamed, begged for help, but what could Cody do? He couldn't even move.

A final arrow stuck in the back of her head, and she reminded him of the Sloth his grandmother gave him. It had Velcro arms, and he hung it on the handle of the kitchen cabinet so he could say hi to it every morning when he had his cereal. Cinnamon Toast Crunch was his favorite. It used to be Fruit Loops, but it changed as he got older.

"What are you doing? Go!" Cole yelled, grabbing him and dragging him toward the house instead of away. Maybe *that was better. Tamara tried to get away, and now she was part of the scenery. Would he become a tree too? A Cody tree. It seemed too surreal to be afraid of. He still wanted to think about cereal. He couldn't bear to think about any of this.*

Cody's back thumped against the wall of the house. He blinked, reality returning for a moment. Cole was staring at him, those blue eyes frantic instead of filled with their usual calm. "We have to watch for him," he said. "Make him come out. Then we can run. From inside, he can just pick us off."

"How do we do that?" Cody asked him.

"I'll make a distraction, try to get his attention, and then duck down. He'll get mad and come out to finish what he started... I hope."

"I thought he wasn't here. I thought he left."

Cole shook his head. "We all did. We saw his truck go, but he must have parked it somewhere and come back. I don't know. It doesn't matter. All that matters now is getting out of here alive."

"Jamie's dead," Cody said quietly.

"I know, I know. It's horrible, bud, but we can't go there now. We'll grieve later. Now we have to make sure we don't die with him, okay? I need you here with me."

"Here with you," Cody said as if noticing him for the first time. Cole sighed and shook his head.

"Just stay here. I'm going to lure him out. When I do...you run. Run sideways...that way...." he pointed. I don't think he can see you from there, and there's no road for his truck. It should take you straight to Mineblock Road. There's the big Halloween store there. It's always crowded. You can get help. You hear me? Cody? Are you hearing me? Come on, bud. Please."

Cody looked at the woods in the direction he had said. He nodded. "I hear you."

Cole licked his lips and nodded back. "Okay. Here goes."

He crept along the side of the house and then stopped, his chest heaving with panicked breaths. Cody watched, waiting to see what he was going to do. Reality struck him then, like a slap to his face. His eyes went wide. "The window!" he yelled to Cole. "Behind you. He uses the windows!"

Cole turned back to look at him, his fear all over his face. He put his finger to his lips to tell Cody to shush. The window beside him shattered outward, and a thick, gnarled arm burst through the glass to cleave Cole's head off with a machete. It tumbled through the air like a volleyball someone failed to hit back and plopped onto the leaves, eyes up, staring back at Cody. He screamed and saw the big man climbing through the window. Truman wore a mask. It was tan with long hair. It looked like it was meant to be Jason Momoa, but it was all wrong... horrifying.

Cody finally found his legs. Apparently his body didn't want to die even if his brain was broken. He turned and bolted in the direction Cole had pointed him. He just had to make it to the road, to the Halloween store. He looked back over his shoulder as he ran, and he saw the enormous man staring back at him through the lopsided eyeholes of his mask. As Cody watched, he took his first step.

"Son, are you with me? Hey. Mr. Wilson. I'm here to help."

Cody was pulled from his memories and found himself staring into the face of Sheriff Sonic. He wasn't fast like the hedgehog, but he didn't need to be. He had a gun, and he was good with it. "You wanna tell me what's going on here? You've got everybody in this store feeling scared, Mr. Wilson. Is this some kind of Halloween prank?"

Cody shook his head. Another animatronic came to life and screamed, jumping up tall, and Cody jumped into the sheriff's arms. "No prank," he said. "He's coming."

The Sheriff hugged him but then gently pushed him back and looked him in the eyes. Cody could still feel the stares of the crowd gathered all around him. They held bags of things they'd already bought or armloads of things they intended to buy. They wore cloaks and plastic armor, which he knew wouldn't help them when Truman

Woodking got there. "Focus on me, son," Sheriff Sonic said. "Who's coming? Tell me what happened?"

Cody looked up and met the sheriff's eyes. He wished they would turn off all the spooky music, the screams, and the laughing clowns. It was making everything worse. "Truman Woodking," he said.

The sheriff seemed less afraid then. His shoulders relaxed, and he sighed. "You gotta stop with old ghost stories, Cody. That old boy ain't never hurt anyone. He comes into town for groceries and to hit the bait and tackle store because he fishes in the river that runs through his property. Other than that, he keeps to his own."

"He does wear that creepy mask," a woman said, pulling her son closer to her and hugging him tightly.

The sheriff sighed again. "That mask? We asked him to wear the mask. If you saw what the boy really looked like, you'd be even more scared. His face is all twisted, but it ain't his fault. He's no monster. He's just a simple boy whose parents passed on. That mask is of his favorite barbarian. Movie came out earlier this year. He wore one of those old plastic ones before that. Boy loves him some Conan but that doesn't make him violent."

Cody shook his head. "My brother Jamie... our friends... he killed them all."

Sheriff Sonic's eyes got hard. "Now, why would he do that? His property is private, Mr. Wilson. It's chained off. No trespassing signs all over. You telling me y'all went and bothered that ol' boy anyhow?"

Cody felt tears rise up and spill over his lower lids to cascade down his face. "We thought he was gone," he cried. "We saw his truck leave."

"So you hooligans thought you would break into his house? You plan on stealing stuff?"

Cody was really crying now. He shook his head. A skeleton nearby came to life and jumped around wildly. He shivered. "No, sir. We just thought it would be cool. The house is so creepy. It's all black and tucked away in the woods. It was just Halloween time fun, I swear. We didn't mean any harm."

"Alright. Then what happened?"

"The windows," Cody said. His eyes started searching the windows of the store as if they also presented danger. "He used the windows and he hunted us."

"He hunted you?"

"They're all dead. They're all dead. It was the windows. He used the windows. They're all dead."

Sheriff Sonic sighed. "Alright. We gotta get you to the hospital. Seems like shock. Can somebody please call his mother? I'm gonna call for backup and head on over to the

Woodking place, see what I can find." He walked over to the girl at the counter as he spoke. Cody followed him with his eyes. He heard a voice behind him then, and whirled around in a panic.

It was another animatronic—a monster with tons of razor-sharp teeth and blaring red eyes. A sign beside it read, *The Game Master.* "Hey, child, let's play a game," it said to him in a booming, deep bassy voice. Cody shook his head and stumbled back a step. The Halloween scare's arm bolted up, and it pointed past him like it was actually trying to warn him of something. As if perfectly timed, the woman from earlier screamed, "Behind you!"

Cody heard other people screaming, too, all warning him. He turned around slowly and saw his nightmare-turned-real. He was staring up at the masked face of Truman Woodking, stiff artificial brown hair jutting out from the sides of his rubber-coated head. Cody could see the Sheriff behind the behemoth, trying to get his gun from his holster. Everything was moving in slow motion.

The blade of Truman's machete glinted in the store's fluorescent lights as it came toward him. Sheriff Sonic's gun boomed repeatedly. Cody's decapitated head still saw Truman's crazed eyes as it soared from his neck. They looked inhuman. He would see nothing else.

Cody, his head, and Truman Woodking all fell to the ground amid the screaming patrons of the Ghostly Halloween superstore, adding to the cacophony of madness the Halloween sounds already created. Sheriff Sonic looked at the bodies and the pooling blood. "My God," he said.

The animatronic jolted to life and pointed its monstrous finger at him. "Let's play a game," it said, its red eyes blaring.

The sheriff snarled with disgust. "Someone turn that thing off," he commanded. "Better yet, get rid of it."

CHAPTER ONE
HAPPY HALLOWEEN

Today.

Kinder stared out the window of the car at the passing trees and streetlights, all decorated for Halloween. His sister, Flower, reached across the backseat and punched him in the arm. "Stop being such a baby," she said.

"I don't like that store. I don't like the animatronics. I don't like jump scares," Kinder fired back. "You know that."

"Because you're a baby," she told him. "You're a scaredy cat. You were like two years old when the Nightwalker scared you. But you're older now, bro. You gotta get over it. They're just plastic and wires. Grow up."

"Flower, be nice to your brother," their mother said from the front passenger seat.

"He doesn't have to like the same things you do," their father said as he drove.

"Can I stay in the car?" Kinder asked.

"Sorry, champ," his father said. "You want a costume for the party with your friends, and we're not picking it for you."

"But–"

"No buts," his mother said. "We understand the store is scary, but just go right past the animatronics and find what you want to wear. Once you have it, you can give it to me, and I'll wait in line. Then you can go back to the car."

Flower rolled her eyes. "Or you can pretend like you're not a loser and just go to a *store*."

"Flower!" her mother scolded.

"Well, he's lame as heck."

"Enough."

"Enough being lame? I know. That's literally what *I'm* saying."

Their dad sighed. "If you don't quit it, no one is going to the Ghostly Halloween Superstore. I'll just turn this thing around and take us all home."

"Mom!" Flower yelled.

"All you have to do is be nice," her mother said.

"She doesn't know how," said Kinder. Flower punched him again. "Ow! Mom!"

"Flower!" their mother barked, turning around in her seat to point at them. "We're really about to not go! Stop it, now."

Flower rolled her eyes and slouched in her seat, pouting. "It's not like I killed his pet or something."

"Again," Kinder mumbled.

"Enough!" their mom scolded. She looked at her husband. "Alright. They can't behave. Do it. Turn around and go home."

Flower's eyes went wide. "No way! Mom! *Please*! I *have* to go. You can't do this! I'll behave okay? Come on. I won't pick on the loser anymore. I promise. Okay?"

"We'll try again another day," their mother said. "There's still time before Halloween."

"No! Mom! I have to go *today*!"

They stopped at a red light, and their father sighed, turning back to glance at them. "Why? Why is it so imperative to go *today*?"

"Today is the first day they're unveiling the reissue of a canceled animatronic that has been out of commission for fourteen years."

"So," her mother said. "We're not buying an animatronic. Those things are way too expensive. They're hundreds of dollars, Flower."

"She doesn't care. She'll probably steal it," Kinder mumbled. He flinched, expecting his sister to punch him again, but she somehow fought the urge in her efforts to get to the Halloween superstore.

"I don't wanna buy it," Flower told them. "I just want to see it when it's released. It's exciting. It was supposed to be the main animatronic for their 2011 line, but it got decommissioned after something crazy happened."

Kinder took his eyes off the window and gazed at her fearfully. "What do you mean? What happened?"

Flower's face looked purely evil. She grinned from ear to ear. "A crazed, deformed woodsman in a mask cleaved a boy's head off right in front of it. He was your age and his blood splashed all over its monstrous face, but the game master just kept pointing and demanding to play his game." She lowered her voice as deep as she could. "Let's play a game," she crooned. "Let's play a game."

Kinder shivered. He shoved her. "Stop it. No. I'm not going in that store. Forget it."

His mother sighed. "Flower, must you frighten your brother? That's not going to get you what you want."

"That *is* what I want," she said wickedly.

"Well, that's it then. We're going home," her father said.

"No! Why? I hate you!" she yelled at her brother, pummeling him with her fists. He covered his head with his arms to deflect her blows.

"Flower!" Her parents were both screaming. Her father pulled the car into the nearest parking lot and slammed it into park. He whirled around and glared at her. "What is wrong with you? We did not raise you like this. I will not tolerate the violence!"

Flower looked past him out the window of the car, and her eyes lit up. "We're here!" she said. She threw her car door open and leaped out.

"What?!" her angry father bellowed. He turned around and saw through the windshield that they were in the parking lot of the newly erected traveling Halloween superstore. Not fifty yards away was the NOW OPEN sign for *Ghostly Halloween*. He growled and grumbled, shaking his head. "Son of a–"

CHAPTER TWO
GHOSTLY HALLOWEEN

"Why do I have to go in?" Kinder complained as his mother dragged him by the arm.

"Because we already had your sister run away, and we need to keep track of you kids. We're not leaving you in the car, so you're out of our sight. We're getting her, getting your costume, and going home."

"And when we do, your sister just might not be allowed to leave again for the next six months."

Kinder's eyes widened with fear. "Please don't do that to me. Grounding her is a punishment for me, not her. Send her somewhere else for six months. That would be better."

"Stop," his mother said firmly. "I don't know why you kids can't just be nice. You'd think we beat you or something. Neither of you has been spanked in your life."

"Maybe that's where we went wrong," her husband said. "Maybe these kids need a good beating."

"That's not funny," she said, scolding him.

"I'm with Mom," Kinder said.

They finished crossing the parking lot and went through the automatic doors of the store. Immediately, crows cawed and scream queens shrieked. Kinder and his mother both jumped. His father just smirked and laughed quietly as they passed through the sensors to make sure no one was stealing.

"Do you see her?" Mom said. "I want to get her and get out of here."

"I don't, but you know she's here somewhere. Why don't you ask someone about that thing she was talking about? What was it called? The Game Master."

Mom looked around and then met her husband's eyes. "Yeah, okay," she agreed. She gave Kinder a gentle shove. "Go find what you want to wear because once we get a hold of your sister, we are leaving right away."

"It's okay, I'll just stay here," he said, staring at the animatronics and the people they made jump and scream. Those people, or at least most of them, laughed after getting scared half to death, but Kinder didn't see the humor. He remembered his first time in one of these stores. The Night Walker was on a track. It actually came for him and he fell and it got to the end and lurched forward, reaching over him with its green bony hands and screaming like the damned. He peed. He cried. He was terrified and humiliated in equal measure and vowed never again. Yet here he was. In previous years, he'd just grabbed a costume at Storemart. He was completely content with that. He didn't need all this.

"No," his father told him with stern eyes. "We're here now. I'm not driving you somewhere else because you don't want to shop at the store you're already in. If you don't buy something here, you don't get a costume unless you make it yourself from whatever you can find at the house."

Kinder sighed. He looked out at an archway where a giant clown chortled and shoved a stick of cotton candy into two girls' faces. The cotton had a severed head in it, and they screamed when they saw it, jumping backwards and giggling when they landed. Gleefully, they ran to the next one. Kinder swallowed a lump in his throat.

"Go on," his mother said, gently nudging him.

Reluctantly, Kinder stumbled forward. He tried to skirt his way around a scarecrow with a jack-o-lantern head and ran into someone's back. "Hey! Watch where the heck you're going!" they yelled at him.

"Sorry," he said quietly with his head down. All around him creatures laughed and howled, bit and reached for him. Killers talked and clowns laughed. Circus music played as well as spooky organ sounds. It was just pure chaos, a cluster of evil, and he hated every second of it. He had never wanted to be home so much in his life.

Kinder didn't even know what he wanted to be. He hadn't given it much thought. He figured he would see something and it would just feel right but nothing in this place felt right to him at all. A giant bat flapped its wings and then closed them over him. He screamed and was about to fight to break free when the wings reopened and let him go. He dove forward and stumbled, sprawling to the floor. Some other kids pointed and laughed at him. He responded with a gesture that would get him in big trouble if his mother saw it, but when he looked around, he didn't see either of his parents. He felt terribly afraid and swallowed a lump in his throat.

Someone extended a hand to help him up. He took it and when they pulled, he realized it was a skeleton hand and he yelped and let go, falling back onto his rump. The boy holding the skeleton hand and his friends all howled with laughter. One even took pictures on his phone, the jerk. Then they ran off excitedly, and Kinder was left alone, staring up at the dark cavernous eyes of a green-skinned witch. He had heard legends of the Witch of the World. She was said to be the Death Digger's mother and he imagined this was exactly what she would look like if she were real, but he supposed there was no way to know for sure. Maybe a real witch would look just like anyone in this store. That thought left him even more frightened, and he looked around for someone who could actually be evil.

"There you are," a voice said as a hand seized the collar of his shirt. He was tugged backward out of sight and into a dark corridor where he couldn't even see the store and the bright lights it offered any longer. He could still hear kids and adults talking, laughing, and screaming, and the sounds of the animatronics going off when people stepped on their start spaces but it sounded dulled, far away. Everything was so dark. "Hello?" he whined. "What is this place? Where am I?"

His sister's face cut through the darkness, and she looked at him, her eyes full of mischief and her smile wicked.

CHAPTER THREE
THE GAME MASTER

"I don't know what you're up to and I don't care," Kinder told his sister as he trembled in the dark of the corridor she had dragged him into. "I just want to get my costume and go home. Besides, Mom and Dad are really mad. You're already gonna be in big trouble. You shouldn't add to it."

She just laughed at him. "Mom and Dad are goodies. That's so boring. I'm not worried about them. What are they gonna do? Send us away?"

"What's this *us* stuff? I didn't do anything. They'll send *you* away."

"Yeah, right. You always end up in trouble, too, and you know it. Where I go, you'll go with me."

"Why do you have to be like this?"

She laughed again. "Like Lady Gaga says, 'I was born this way'."

"What even is this place? It's too dark. I don't like it, Flower. I just want to go back out there with everyone."

Another laugh. "We will soon enough." She put her arm around him and turned him, leading him down a tunnel of mirrors. A she looked at them, lights blinked on over each one, showing him a distorted image of himself and his sister. As they passed, the light blinked off, there was a moment of darkness, and then the next light blinked on to show the next strange mirror image.

"Is this why Mom and Dad couldn't see you anywhere?" he asked, his voice quivering. "Were you hiding in here the whole time?"

Flower laughed once more. "I wasn't hiding. I was exploring. How creepy are the mirrors and the lights in here? Isn't it awesome?"

"No. I want to go back out there. Where is the end?"

"I don't know. It's crazy. It's like it goes on forever. I think it's some kind of optical illusion," she said with a giggle.

"No. Flower, that's terrible. I want to get out. I can't breathe. Please."

"Ugh. It's time for you to grow up, little brother," she said, pushing him from behind. He tripped and yelped, waving his arms in the dark for something to help him keep from falling. Flower laughed again and caught his shirt, tugging him upright. "See? What would you do without me?"

"I'd be safe and calm and life would be peaceful," he said with a scowl. "And stop calling me little brother like you're so much older than me. You're not even one full year older, Flower."

"Well, you wouldn't know it, the way you always act like a baby," she snapped back. He was gonna yell at her again, but they pushed through a tent flap and wound up back out on the sales floor under the bright lights and amid the chaos of the Halloween sounds. Part of him wanted to turn and go back in now that he knew there was nothing in there that could hurt him.

"See, you didn't die," his sister told him.

"No thanks to you."

"Hey! I kept you from falling."

"You were the *reason* I was falling!"

"Toe-may-toe, toe-mah-toe," she said. "Look. There it is."

Kinder looked up and saw, upon a pedestal before him, the most terrifying animatronic he'd ever seen. It was hunched and covered in leathery hide that was riddled with warts and pustules. Its gnarled bones jutted in all directions, and its eyes blazed red as it stared at him. Its mechanical mouth opened and closed with a whirring tape sound, and it said, "Welcome. I'm the Game Master. Let's play a game!"

CHAPTER FOUR
THE WINDOW

Kinder didn't like this thing one bit. He didn't like the store, the sounds, the mechanical monsters, and at least at this moment, he didn't like his sister either. "Okay, you saw it," he said, fear evident in his voice. "Let's go find Mom and Dad and go home now. You had your fun."

Flower shook her head. The way she smiled and her eyes were glistening with madness, she looked like she could have been one of the monsters herself. He'd seen her get that look before. Sometimes, Flower did really bad things. She hurt animals and people, and she enjoyed it. He tried not to be a part of it, but also did his best to keep her from getting in serious trouble because she was his sister, but there was definitely something wicked in her. There were times, times like this, where he was truly afraid of his own sibling.

"We can't go just yet, little brother. That was just the automatic phrase activated by the motion sensor. We have to press the button to play the actual game."

Kinder swallowed hard. "I don't want to play the game. I want to get my costume and go home."

"Baby."

"Call me what you want. I don't care. You're a real bully sometimes."

Flower rubbed her eyes like she was crying and did her best to impersonate a sobbing baby. Kinder just glared at her. "I want to go," he said firmly.

"We'll go as soon as you step over there, press the button, and play the Game Master's game."

"No." He went to walk away, and she grabbed him, pulling him back. "Stop it!" he snapped.

"I will, when you press the button and play the game."

"Why don't you do it?"

She laughed. "Because some people online say it's cursed and I want to see for myself."

"What the heck, Flower?! I'm not gonna be your stupid test subject."

"Then we'll be here forever, and you're never going home. I know the place. I can hide us until it's closed, and even the workers have gone home."

"I saw that movie. No, thank you."

"Then do it."

"Why do they say it's cursed?"

"I told you why in the car. The Wood King."

"The Wood King?" He looked at her, hoping she was just telling another story and trying to scare him.

Her grin widened. Flower nodded. "That was his actual name. Truman Woodking. He lived in a dark black house in the middle of the woods, and he wore a terrifying mask.

A few years before you were born, he killed a bunch of kids and followed the last one here... well, not here specifically, but to a Ghostly Halloween Superstore where he chopped the boy's head clean off right in front of this animatronic. The Sheriff shot him several times and killed the Wood King, but the Game master just kept going even after they unplugged it. "Let's play a game....let's play a game....let's play a game..."

"There's no way that's true," Kinder told her, but his gaze was focused on the horrible animatronic monster on the pedestal before him.

"It is.... Look it up. They retired the animatronic before almost anyone bought one. The few that were sold are worth a gazillion dollars, or at least they were before the reissue."

"If that was true, then why would they bring it back?" he asked, folding his arms in front of him.

Flower ran her fingers together before his face, rubbing her thumb on her middle finger. "Money. Bringing it back brings people back. It's legendary, man, and it's been long enough. It's almost fifteen years since the murders."

"Still..."

"Still, nuthin'. Come on. I'm sure it's just a regular animatronic. Just press the button, let's see what it does, and we can go. I promise."

"If you're so sure it's fine, you press it."

Her response was to shove him from behind, causing him to stumble forward. He windmilled his arms and tried not to fall, but stepped right onto the button. Kinder froze, his heart seized by fear. He glanced down at his foot and then his eyes trailed up to stare into the red glowing orbs of the monster's gaze. Flower stepped off to the side to watch from a safe position. Other people were watching too, gathering around.

"No one was courageous enough to press it yet," a stocky guy in a Michael Myers shirt said to him.

Why was it taking so long? Kinder wondered. He was beginning to sweat, his nerves getting the best of him. "It doesn't seem like it does *anything*," he said to the onlookers. He stepped back, taking his foot off the button.

As soon as he did, creepy organ music blared to life, and smoke poured from machines on either side of the animatronic. A loud scream rang out and the thing leaned forward to make eye contact, the bright red eyes blazing even brighter, so bright that Kinder had to squint and shield his own. Some of the people watching gasped. He wondered if his parents were among them. Deep down, he hoped they were, and they would grab him and forcefully whisk him away so he wouldn't have to be a coward for leaving, just a kid in trouble. That seemed better because kids loved Flower despite the things she did.

"Let's play a game!" the Game master boomed. "It's called…. Window!"

"Window?" Kinder repeated sheepishly.

The thing's arm shot up, and it pointed its gnarled hand past him. "Look!" it commanded. Kinder could already hear the crowd *ooooo*ing and gasping. He even saw Flower with her mouth pried open in silent awe. What could be behind him? He was terrified, but he knew he had to look. He had to see.

Slowly, Kinder turned around and sucked in air, his body going rigid. There was a window right there, hovering in the air, nothing above it or below it or to either side. It didn't make any sense how it could be suspended there with no support. He could see the shine of the overhead lights, proving that the front was a glass pane just like the windows at home. On the other side of the window, he could see woods, trees, and autumn leaves raining down upon yellowed grass. Was it another optical illusion like the endless tunnel of mirrors?

"Touch the window!" the Game Master commanded.

"Don't do it," someone from the crowd told him. Kinder knew they were probably right, but curiosity got the best of him. He reached out with shaking fingers and gently touched the impossible pane of glass that hovered before him. The moment he did, the glass shattered outward, and onlookers screamed. A masked man with scraggly, long brown hair, reached thick, muscled arms through the window and grabbed Kinder by the hair and shirt. Before anyone could even move to help, Kinder was dragged through the impossible window and then just as it had appeared... it was gone.

CHAPTER FIVE
OOPS

"What did you do? What is this? I know you had something to do with this," Flower's mother yelled at her as she pushed her way through the crowd. "Where the hell is your brother, Flower? I'm not even playing with you right now. What did you do?"

"I don't—I—I uh, he ....I don't..."

A stranger answered for her, walking up to stand before her parents. She knew she was dead meat, but she didn't even care. That was the most horrifying, and amazing thing she'd ever seen in her life. The curse was real. The ghost of Truman Woodking was real, and the Wood King dragged her brother into...where? She didn't even know.

"The animatronic never should have been brought back," the man told her parents. "It's cursed. That boy is gone."

"Gone? What do you mean, '*Gone*'? Her frantic mother bellowed like she could have been one of the animatronics for the season.

A Goth kid with white face paint, black lipstick, and a C.A. Baynam shirt approached. He nodded toward the pile of broken glass on the floor, pointing with a spiked wristbanded arm and a hand full of rings with eyes and hooks on them. "A window appeared in the air and a freaking monster came through it."

A blonde girl holding a Buzz Lightyear costume chimed in. "It grabbed the boy and pulled him through, and then the window just... it disappeared."

"What do you mean it disappeared?!" Flower's mother was screaming now. She was hysterical, irrational. Flower had to hold back the laughter that wanted to bubble out of her mouth. "Children don't just disappear through magic windows! Windows don't just appear and disappear! They're either there or they aren't!"

The woman started cursing, and Flower had only heard her mother curse a few times in her lifetime. It almost never happened, but boy was it happening now. She was really losing it. Flower had to cover her mouth with her hand and hope her furious mother didn't notice her laughing. With the amount of rage her mother was showing, it could have ended up being the first time she'd ever hit her.

She watched her father trying to console her and calm her, but it wasn't working at all. "You call the police!" she yelled. "You call the police and you tell them someone took my son! He's here somewhere. I don't know what kind of awful trick this is, but it's not okay."

"It was him," a woman told her. "It was Truman Woodking."

"The Wood King isn't real!" Her mother was red-faced and screaming.

"Actually, he is... err... was," said the manager as she parted the crowd to approach. She wore a button-down shirt with pumpkins and bats on it and had round glasses. "I worked at the store it happened at. I was there that day. I was only a cashier back then, but I'll never forget it as long as I live. I petitioned to fight the rerelease of the Game Master, but money speaks louder than I do, I guess."

Flower's mother lost her fury and started to cry. Her chest heaved and shook, and her husband held her close to him, his arm around her shoulders. "You're telling us that there's a real madman killer on the loose and he has our boy?" he asked the manager.

She shook her head. "No. I don't know. I mean, I saw the sheriff gun him down. He definitely died."

Flower's dad released her mom and stepped forward. "Well, then let's do it again. Maybe I can go through the window and get him back if it's real."

"That's a bad idea," someone called out, but he didn't listen. He stepped forward and stomped hard on the button. Nothing happened. Now he was feeling his wife's fury. "Alright, everyone!" he yelled. "If it's real, where is it? Where's your magic window? Where's my son?"

Everyone was murmuring and whispering. Flower ducked into the dark hallway of mirrors to escape the wrath of her parents. If they found her, she was going to be in the worst trouble she'd ever been in. She didn't know a ghost was going to whisk her brother off to God knows where. She hoped... but she didn't *know*.

"It's not working at all," the manager said to her father outside. Flower huddled in the dark and just listened to the distant voices. "Maybe whatever happened blew the circuit or something."

"Then get a different one," he commanded. "Build a new one. You have more in boxes, right? The whole point is to sell these stupid things, isn't it? Go get one."

The manager sighed. "Look. It's burnt. It's not the animatronic. It's the electricity to the whole area."

"Well, the lights are still on, so some electric is working," he barked. "Set it up where the power is working. I don't care what you do. Just find my damn son."

"Yes, sir. We'll try. We'll do whatever we can. In the meantime, I have already notified the police of the situation, and they're on their way."

Holy poop nuggets, Flower thought. She was really in a big mess this time. This wasn't Mrs. Bullworth's poodle. This was Kinder. "Crap," she said quietly.

CHAPTER SIX
THE WOODS

K inder was soaring through the air, screaming. Then he hit the ground hard with an "Oomph."

Looking up at the surrounding trees, he immediately remembered how he got there and quickly scrambled to his feet in a panic. He looked around, his senses on high alert for danger.

About fifty feet away, the mammoth that was Truman Woodking stood among the trees, staring at him through his mask that had warped more over time, one side drooping like it was made of dripping wax. Kinder's body hurt, but he trembled with fear. The Wood King was massive. He blended in with the trees. He might as well have been one of them. In the hand he hadn't grabbed Kinder and pulled him through the window with, he held a rusted old machete. Kinder wasn't ready to take chances that the old thing wasn't sharp. He imagined a slash from an arm that powerful could make a butter knife chop a head clean off.

Without a sound, the Wood King stepped toward him. That was his cue. Kinder turned and took off running through the trees. He felt like he was at a terrible disadvantage. This was Truman's home, his property. Surely he knew it like the back of his hand. Where could Kinder run to that the giant wouldn't be able to find him?

As he ran, Kinder couldn't help but look back over his shoulder. He needed to know that the man was still following. Was he a man? He was dead, wasn't he? If he looked back and didn't see him anymore, he would have to assume that he veered off for a reason, that he knew a shortcut and planned to cut Kinder off somewhere. Then he would need to change course to be sure he didn't run into those heavily muscled arms. He didn't need anyone to tell him that would be a death sentence.

Kinder still couldn't wrap his brain around the fact that this was even real. How was it possible? His sister obviously suspected it, and that's why she made him the guinea pig. He was mad at her, but needed to focus on survival. He would say bad words for the first time in his life when he got back home and saw her again. First, he needed to make sure he did that.

Every time he looked back, the beast was there, walking casually, like there was no rush. He knew he would catch his prey eventually and wasn't stressed about it. *Can't say I feel the same,* Kinder thought. *I'm very stressed, so very stressed.*

He hated running aimlessly through the seemingly infinite trees that all looked the same. He was without a doubt as lost as lost could be. Kinder wasn't even sure these woods actually led anywhere other than the Woodking house. It wasn't a real place, right? So maybe any direction he chose would lead him to the same place. Maybe that's why Truman walked without a care in the world. Could he be hurt if Kinder were to find a weapon? He could definitely hurt Kinder. The aches in his bones and muscles told him that clearly enough. He remembered the way Truman's arms came through the solid glass and yanked him through like he was little more than paper.

Kinder didn't know the rules, but he knew for sure that he wasn't ready to die. He kept looking back to be sure that Truman was following him. A day ago, he would have thought that seeing the Wood King behind him would be terrible, but now he took a strange comfort in it. At least he knew where the monster was.

He didn't understand how someone that big could move that quietly, though. Maybe it was a testament to being dead. Kinder, on the other hand, was very much alive and ran loudly through the wet leaves that scattered the muddy ground, panting like a dog in heat.

He was getting tired, and that scared him. He had a feeling that a man like Truman Woodking didn't get tired even when he was alive. If Kinder couldn't run anymore, he was dead. He looked around for any place he could go to catch his breath and rid himself of the stitch in his side, but all he saw were trees. Their tangled limbs and raining orange leaves managed to even block out most of the sky. This was a true nightmare.

He looked back again and saw the Wood King stop and cock his head sideways like a golden retriever, looking at him through the warped eyeholes of the dropping mask. "Leave me alone!" Kinder screamed at him. "Go away!"

Truman's silent footsteps resumed.

Kinder jumped when a murder of crows burst from the trees he ran through, fluttering into the air with a chaotic flapping of black wings on either side of him. "How do I get out?!" he screamed, tears in his eyes.

Then he saw the answer. Up ahead was another window just like the one that led him there, hovering in mid-air as if it was plastered in the middle of an invisible wall. If he got here through a window, he could get back through one too, right? At least, that was his hope. He pumped his arms that much harder, driven now that he had hope.

As he neared the window, he could see through it to the interior of a Ghostly Halloween superstore, patrons walking past the window unawares. He screamed as he ran, and waved his arms, but they didn't seem to see or hear him.

Then he saw someone turn and look through. He must have been the one to create the window as Kinder had in his own store. He wanted to tell them to back away, but he already knew they couldn't hear him. He pushed his exhausted body even harder.

He was close then, nearing the floating window suspended between trees, colored leaves floating slowly down around it.

Then there was a blink. A flash of color. Suddenly, the Wood King was there right before the window. This time, he plunged his other arm, rusted blade first, through the window, shattering the glass outward into the store.

Kinder skidded to a halt, and doubled over, breathing hard, but kept his eyes on the window. He watched as Truman's rusty blade cleaved the head off the man standing in a Ghostly Halloween superstore somewhere. When he pulled his blade back through the demolished window, blood sprayed the surrounding trees. The severed head spun in the air, and Kinder caught the look of surprise in the dead man's eyes. He could see the people in the store, frantic and screaming, but he didn't hear a sound, just the quiet chirping of birds, the buzz of insects, and the soft patter of falling leaves joining their brethren.

The window disappeared like it had never been there, and the Wood King turned around to face him, his rusted blade still dripping crimson. Kinder didn't wait to see Flower to say his first bad word. Even though he felt like he just needed to lie in the wet leaves for the next four hours, he turned to his left and forced his body to run.

CHAPTER SEVEN
A LEAD?

Flower sat in the dark and watched her parents and everyone in the store lose their minds over Kinder's disappearance. "What do you mean it doesn't work?" her father screamed. "So then, where the hell is my son?"

"I-I don't know. I'm sorry," said the manager.

"Sorry doesn't cut it. If you had some weird magic trick with this damn thing that made my kid disappear, you need to figure out how to get him back!"

"I'm sorry. I know. We're trying, but sir, we've plugged it in at three different outlets now. It does nothing.. I-I think it's fried."

"That is unacceptable."

"I know. I don't know what to say. I've never had anything like that happen. I don't think anyone has. We tried a different Game Master, straight out of the box, and we did it right in front of you. It did nothing but say its preprogrammed phrases."

"This is insane," Flower's mother said, crying. Flower chuckled at this but clamped her hand over her mouth to keep it quiet. "Windows don't appear out of thin air, and children don't disappear."

An employee came up and said, "The police are here."

The manager sighed with relief. "Oh, thank God. I don't know if they can help find the boy, but they can definitely help deal with his parents. I work retail. I don't get paid enough for this."

Flower watched two officers come over. She listened as the manager explained the situation to them, and her parents kept interrupting and yelling about things. Her mother turned on the waterworks and began sobbing. She felt like giving the woman an award. Sure, she was upset, but she wasn't that hysterical before the police arrived. Flower couldn't help but wonder if her parents would have felt the same if it had been her who went through the window. She imagined not. Kinder was the good one....the weak one. Still, he *was* her brother. She didn't think that they wouldn't be able to get him back, or she wouldn't have made him do it.. She would have pushed a different kid towards it to see what happened.

One of the police officers made everyone get back, and he was roping off the scene. The other walked near her hiding place and called someone. "Nina, it's me. It's happened here, too. I think this is real. Truman Woodking is back somehow. I just heard from Sylvester in Tacoma. They have all the evidence they need over there. No mysterious disappearance. Guy got his head cut clean off in the store before the window disappeared. Tons of witnesses. It's a disaster over there. You want to come yourself? I can meet you." He sighed. "But I like you better than working with Owen. Yes, I know he's a genius, but he doesn't like to follow rules, Nina. Fine. okay. Just tell him to be quick."

Flower's mouth was wide open when she watched the police officer thrust his phone back into his pocket and saunter back over to the manager of the store. "I need to see your security tapes," she heard him say.

In the dark, Flower pulled her phone out of her pocket and opened up her internet browser. She searched for Truman Woodking and discovered that the original slaying happened in the mountains of western North Carolina. She was already in North Carolina. She just had to figure out exactly where the Woodkings lived. She saw the woods through the window. It was a real place. That's where her brother was, and if she wanted to get him back, that's where she needed to go. She chewed on her lip. She wasn't sure how to get there. She couldn't very well go up to her parents and tell them they needed to go drive around the mountains looking for Kinder. They probably wouldn't even hear what she was saying. They would just yell at her for making him disappear in the first place. Grown-ups were always too focused on the problems themselves and not the solutions.

Whoever the cop was talking to on the phone was sending someone named Owen, who seemed to know something about the Wood King. Maybe he would say the location or Flower could convince him to let her tag along if he decided to go himself. Either way, she hoped something happened fast. She hated waiting. Waiting was boring.

CHAPTER EIGHT
THE CHASE

Kinder's mind screamed for him to run, but his body screamed for a break. He felt like he was nearing collapse, but he fought against it. He had to. Each time he looked back, the giant was there, staring through his weird eyeholes, cutting things out of his way with his murderous machete.

There were pros and cons to what just happened. The obvious con was that someone just lost their head. The pro was that there were more windows, and if Kinder could find one, then he could still get back home and away from the blood-spattered psycho maniac on his heels.

The problem with that was that Truman seemed to blink to wherever the window was when someone touched it. Following the Game Master's command and putting your fingers on that phantom glass, summoned the Wood King from wherever he was. This was especially troublesome because it meant that for Kinder to reach a window and escape, he was going to have to go through Truman Woodking and his machete. There was literally no way around it.

For now, he kept running. He wished there was a way to know where the next window was going to show up or when, but he had no idea. It seemed to be completely random. It was all controlled by the animatronic. It must have been happening in stores all over the country. How many? He could only imagine. A lot of people were going to die today. He just wanted to make sure that he wasn't one of them.

The lights were fading, and the woods were growing dark. It left Kinder feeling even more scared than he already was. He felt like he needed to rest, like he wasn't going to be able to run much longer, but he knew he couldn't stop. The Wood King was still behind him.

And then he wasn't.

Kinder looked, his eyes darting through the trees. It was like the giant man just disappeared. Kinder's mouth fell open when he realized he probably did. Another window must have opened. This was another double-edged sword. It meant he had the chance to hide and catch his breath, but it meant another store activated their Game Master, and another opportunity to get back home was lost. What would happen when the last window was shattered? Would he be stuck here forever? Was this even a real pace or some ghost realm that existed in the in-between space? If that was the case, maybe it was only accessible via the windows the Game Master opened. That was a terrifying thought.

Kinder just wanted to go home. He wanted to break down crying and just lie down in the leaves, but he knew Truman would be back and looking for blood. He had to push himself just a little bit longer while the monster was otherwise occupied. He looked around frantically, trying to see where he could go. There was nothing: no holes in trees, no overhangs, no caves, no cabins, nothing. His shoulders shook with silent sobs. How long did he have? How long before he looked over his shoulder and saw the Wood King again, his machete dripping with blood?

He wanted to scream.

Kinder turned in a slow circle looking for something—anything—but all there was were trees and eternally falling leaves. His eyes widened. *The leaves!*

There were so many. They were everywhere. Maybe they would be enough. He started shoveling them to the side and created a large mound. He looked back nervously, then looked left and right. Truman still hadn't returned. His heart was pounding in his thin chest. He lay down, the frozen ground sending chills through his spine, and he hurried to pull the leaves over himself. He couldn't breathe. *Hurry. Hurry. Must hurry.*

Kinder got himself covered and then heard breathing, and he stopped, falling still beneath the leaves. He felt like one of his shoes was still uncovered, and hoped to God that the Wood King couldn't see it. *Please.*

He felt the leaves moving as big steps shoved them aside or tramped them down. It gave him a new fear. Truman didn't have to discover his hiding place to step on him with his tree trunk legs. Kinder held his breath, squeezed his eyes shut, and silently begged for the giant to move on and go look somewhere else. As much as it would further limit his options for getting home, Kinder wished a window would open and take the monster away.

But his prayers weren't answered. The Wood King didn't move, but Kinder could hear the giant's breathing, hoarse and wet. He was still there, just standing nearby, still... waiting. *Go!*

Every second seemed to last for an eternity. Maybe it actually was, he wondered. He didn't know if time worked the same here. He could make it back to his world and find out he was now an old man. He didn't want to miss out on life. All he had so far was his tumultuous childhood with Flower. Kinder always had dreams of getting married and having children of his own, of making movies and writing books. He wanted to go to dances and stand in the back and feel sad and not dance while everyone else had fun, like the relatable kids did in the movies he watched. He wanted to go to parties and not know how to talk to people there, and walk around rubbing his arms until it was time to go home. He had dreams.

Kinder wanted to scream at the unmoving, heavily breathing giant and say, "I didn't break into your house!

I had nothing to do with why you're angry, and I would never do that. Just leave me alone." He knew the answer would be a rusted blade to the throat, though, so he kept his mouth sealed tight.

The breathing continued. Kinder was finding it hard to go on without breathing himself. His face and throat burned. He was so scared to breathe, though. He thought the leaves would move with the rise and fall of his chest and Truman would see it. That was what he was waiting for, some sign, the littlest thing to tell him where the boy was. Kinder knew it. He refused to give it to him. He would hold his breath until he died before he would let that monster kill him. *This is what your prank got me. Are you happy now, Flower?* She probably was, he thought. She wasn't like him. She wasn't like anyone. Flower had a darkness in her, and he knew his parents saw it. He watched the way they looked at her and acted around her. They were afraid of her. Sometimes he feared they would send Flower away. Despite what he had said earlier, and how crazy she was, she was all he had. He didn't know what he would do without his sister. He needed her.

Footsteps.

Leaves crunched. Truman was finally moving on, going to look for him elsewhere. He wanted so badly to breathe, but he knew he had to wait just a few moments longer.

Kinder's fingers clawed at the dirt beneath the leaves as his lungs screamed for air. Then at last, he sat up like a zombie emerging from the earth, scattering leaves and dirt everywhere. He sucked in air and and released it slowly over and over as his eyes combed the surrounding trees for any sign of his would-be killer. There were none. Kinder actually laughed quietly, and fell back onto the ground. He was gone. He was really gone. Oh, thank God, he was gone.

Then a shadow fell over him. Kinder looked up and gasped.

CHAPTER NINE
THE MEETING

The whole place was chaos. People were yelling, messing with animatronics, and the electricity; police were conducting interviews and watching security camera footage. But Flower didn't care about any of that. She was just focused on one person—that cop who made the phone call.

She heard someone call him Mikey, but she didn't care if his name was Doodoo McPoopybutt. She only cared that he knew something about what was going on and he might be able to help her get her brother back. This was her fault. It wasn't an accident. She meant to scare him and maybe watch him get traumatized and possibly a little hurt before she stepped in to rescue him from the pain she caused, but she never meant for this. Her parents didn't like her, and other kids were afraid of her. She had to admit to herself that Kinder was all she really had in this world. If anything ever happened to him, she would be completely and utterly alone, and she didn't much care for the idea of that.

She watched the cop head down a hall. Flower poked her head out, looked both ways, and shot out of her hiding place in a crouch, running behind him. She looked over her shoulder to see if anyone was watching her, but they were all otherwise occupied. Heck, her parents were so concerned with what happened to Kinder that they hadn't even realized yet that she was also gone. Would they even care if they did?

Sometimes, Flower wished that the Witch of the World had given her to the Death Digger as a baby. Her parents didn't know she was different back then, and they still loved her and would have been crushed. It would have served them right.

This line of thought made her wonder about the Wizard of the Woods. If he was real and he really controlled what happened in all the woodland, then he knew all about the Wood King and allowed it. That said something about the kind of being he was. The magic users who worked together to rule this planet seemed to be less than nice in their methods. Flower couldn't really blame them. If she had that kind of power, she would impose all kinds of suffering upon the world. Too bad she didn't, she thought as she looked back at her parents.

Then she disappeared down the hall and followed the policeman around a corner and down another dark hall to a door marked 'Exit'. He pushed the door open, and she waited, peeking around the corner of the wall. When he pulled out his phone and she felt like he was distracted enough not to notice her, she hurried through the slowly closing door and ran to a tree that she used for cover.

The officer hung up the phone as a yellow Lamborghini pulled up. Flower's mouth was agape. Who would be driving that?

The man who got out was the definition of a cool guy. He had on sunglasses at night, had purple hair, and a matching purple suit with a yellow tie and matching yellow loafers. He didn't look as happy or excited to be involved in whatever was happening as Flower was to see him.

"Owen," the police officer said, heading over and shaking his hand.

"Mikey. How is this happening?"

"I know it's crazy, but I think when my dad killed Truman, his soul connected to the animatronic. It opened some kind of window to his personal afterlife."

"You're right, that's crazy."

"We've been in contact with other precincts and Ghostly Halloween stores, and some people were killed right then and there before the window closed, but in this store, a boy was taken, and we have to assume he's still alive somewhere."

"Somewhere? I think we know where. You know, Mikey... I have a life. I have a company, a damn nice house, a cool car, a really cute dog and a beautiful wife. Chasing after the already dead killer who murdered my brother when I was a kid is not my idea of a good time."

"Hey, I didn't ask for you," Mikey said. "I called Nina. Something didn't sit right about this case with her. After Tamara died, she never let it go. I thought she would jump at the chance for some answers, but she said she was ..... Indisposed and couldn't come."

Owen sighed. "I know about her cancer, Mikey. She's been fighting for years. This is her third bout with it. Sometimes I think the chemo and radiation are worse than the disease."

"Yeah."

"Anyway, that's why I'm here. She does want the answers. She asked me to come. I'm here for her."

"Fair enough. So what do you want to do?"

Flower was asking herself the same question. There wasn't much of a backseat in a Lambo, but she couldn't let these two leave without her. Wherever they planned to go, she just knew it would lead to her brother. She was going with them, and that was the end of it, but she wasn't strong enough to force them if they said no. *Maybe I can squeeze?* She had to try.

While the men were engaged in their conversation, Flower ran past the still-open door and climbed into the car. Her heart sank immediately. *Crap.*

The two seats went all the way to the back. There was literally nowhere to hide. Maybe she could pop the trunk but there was no way the men wouldn't notice. She sighed in frustration and decided, to heck with it. She sat down in the passenger seat and secured her seatbelt. Then she waited. She listened to the rest of the conversation happening outside.

"I can't leave. I'm on duty. I have to stay, but I'll try to keep an eye on this place in case the boy manages to find his way back, or…. Something else does."

Owen sighed. "Alright, Mikey, good luck. I guess I'm heading out to the woods where our siblings were killed. If he's really a ghost and you're right about it being his afterlife, I don't know that I'll find anything when I get there."

"I know, but we have to try."

"I hate that damn house, you know."

"I know. I do too."

"Can't you just get like a ton of police to go over there?"

"I could try, but I have a feeling that no one will believe me outside of my dad, and he's retired, so that wouldn't be all that helpful."

Owen sighed again. "Alright. I want to get this over with. I'll call you if I find anything."

"You have your gun?"

"Way the world is now, I never leave home without it."

"I feel that. Be safe out there, please. I don't want to have to call your mom like my dad did."

"Got it."

Flower watched through the windshield of the Lambo as Officer Mikey sauntered his way back into the building with a wag of his hips like he was a cowboy. Owen gave one last sigh and climbed into his car. As he closed the door, he immediately turned to Flower and said, "No. Nope. What are you doing? Tonight is not the night for free rides in the Lambo. You gotta get out."

Flower didn't look at him. She kept her eyes forward. "My brother is the one who went through the mirror. If there's any chance of you getting him back, I'm going. Do not try to stop me because I am not leaving this car, and if you try to make me, I swear I will scream with everything I have."

"If you get me in trouble, there will be no one to save your brother."

"Then I suggest you drive."

He sat there a moment as if he were mulling it over in his mind. He glared at her as he did, his eyes angry.

"Drive," she said again.

Owen grumbled, started the car, and drove away from the store. "You better not get yourself killed," he said as the Lambo roared down the highway like a hungry dinosaur.

CHAPTER TEN
THE WIZARD OF THE WOODS

"Who the heck are you?" Kinder asked the bearded old man staring down at him with a broken-toothed smile.

"I walk the woods in every plane," the man said. He took Kinder's hand and helped him up. "I am the connection between this world and yours."

Kinder's eyes widened. "You're the Wizard of the Woods. You're real!"

The old man nodded. "There are other people here. There were four, but one of them has perished, I'm sad to say."

"I watched someone die before they even came through the window."

The old man nodded. "Yes. That was the fate of most. He looked for five that resemble the original five. There is a reason you are alive. His soul isn't just attached to that mechanical Halloween decoration. It is attached to the event. He needs to relive it, to set it right, so I've allowed him a window to your world in order to do that."

Kinder's face contorted with anger. "You *let* him do this? This is your doing? Why would you do that? People are dying?!"

The man showed no emotion. "People are always dying. Death is a part of life, son. I do not make my decisions based on that. Nature goes beyond that. Nature is mine. An unnatural spirit unable to rest in my woods is something I need to settle. So, I'm allowing him the chance to put himself to rest and, in turn, allow my woods to return to peace."

Kinder shook his head. He looked over his shoulder nervously, scanning the trees for the killer he knew would be returning soon. "And what part do I play in this little game of yours?"

"Funny you should say that. I guess I am the true game master after all, aren't I? You, Kinder, are the new Cody. You're the final boy."

Kinder's heart started thundering. He swallowed hard. "Cody still died."

"He did, but so did Truman. That's the problem. If you watch scary movies, then you know that's not how it goes. Either the final boy lives or everyone dies, and the killer is victorious. Never do they both perish. It wasn't supposed to end like that. For him to rest, this needs to end differently. This time... one of you must live. So you have full disclosure, it doesn't matter to me which one."

Kinder glared with boiling anger. "If I do survive this, I hope I never see you again."

The old man shrugged. "I have a feeling you shall. Now go, run.... Find the others." Cody shook his head with annoyance, but he did what he was told. He didn't feel like he had a choice. Game or not, he wanted to live. Living meant running. He looked back as he ran, and the old man was gone. Kinder growled. He was getting really tired of people disappearing.

He half-wondered if he found the other victims, if they would up and disappear on him too. He wouldn't know until he found them. Another look back showed him Truman Woodking stalking behind him. Just as he feared, the machete in his hand dripped fresh crimson onto the softly falling leaves of Autumn snow.

CHAPTER ELEVEN
GETTING TO KNOW EACH OTHER

"If you're tagging along, at least make yourself useful," Owen said with a sideways glance at Flower.

"I'm not doing anything gross," she snapped.

He looked repulsed, like he was bordering on vomiting all over his steering wheel. "I'm married and have a kid. I mean, help me end this. Tell me exactly what happened at the Ghostly Halloween."

"Oh," Flower said, looking a little embarrassed and turning away. She didn't think she was out of line. She didn't know this man, but she knew men. She watched the news and doomscrolled social media all the time. Reddit and TikTok were full of horror stories. She just wanted to be safe. She cleared her throat and settled further into her seat.

"Well, I heard all these ghost stories about the Game Master's return, right? There's YouTube videos about haunted animatronics. My favorite influencer, Lyssey Noel, did an episode where she showed haunted Halloween decorations and told their stories. I wanted to see if they were true."

Owen glanced over at her, then turned his eyes immediately back to the road. "And?"

"And what?" she asked with a shrug behind her shoulder strap seatbelt. "I waited in the tunnel of mirrors for my brother to be near and then I dragged him through so he got scared and disoriented. Then I brought him back out into the contrasting bright light of the store, and when he was scared and flustered, I pushed him."

"You *pushed* him?"

She turned her nose up and crossed her arms. "Don't judge me. You don't even know me. Yes. I pushed him. He wouldn't do it if I just asked him. He's scared of everything."

Owen shook his head slightly and mumbled something, which earned him another angry glare. "Well, I wasn't going to step on it myself!" Flower barked. "What if it was real and a ghost like killed me or something?"

"So you figured, I know...I'll sacrifice my brother."

She sighed and looked down at her lap. "No. I don't know. I didn't think anything near what actually happened would happen. I just thought something would scare him and make him pee his pants, and I'd get a good laugh."

"You're evil."

"Ugh. Now you sound like my parents and teachers, and everyone. I don't care about your opinion."

Owen took a deep breath and let it out slowly. "So what did happen?"

Flower shivered at the thought, still unable to wrap her head around it. "The Game Master said to play Window."

"Window?" For some reason, this seemed to make Owen nervous and she eyed him with curiosity.

"Yeah. Why? Is that significant?"

"I don't know," he sighed. He jerked the wheel, and the car swerved to avoid a fear-stricken bunny who was staring at them through its red eyes, ears straight up like antennae. Flower frowned with disappointment. If she had been driving, she would have found out what it sounded like when she ran over the frightened creature, the way the car moved, and whether or not she could hear it cry out or hear the bones crunch. It would have been a fun experiment. Her concentration was broken when he said, "They went to the house after Truman was killed. That's when they found my brother and the others. When they did, many of the windows of that creepy, lopsided, night-black house were broken and they were broken outward from the inside. It seemed like he hid within and killed those kids by using the windows."

Flower threw her arms up. "Well, that makes horrifying sense, so thanks for that."

"It makes more sense than a kid throwing her own brother to the wolves. Tell me what happened next."

She paused for a moment to stare at him with anger burning in her irises, but then she sighed and said, "The Game Master pointed over Kinder's shoulder like the threat was behind him, and if what you just said is true, that makes sense also."

"Jesus." He swallowed a lump that seemed to have formed in his throat. "Then what?"

Flower shrugged again. "Kinder turned around to look behind him, and there really was a window there. It was the craziest thing. It just hung in the air, attached to nothing, but I could see through it and on the other side were the woods, just like in the legend."

Owen growled then and took a turn to be the one glaring angrily. "It isn't legend, you fool child. It's real life. My brother is *dead*!"

She rolled her eyes at him. "Wow, so we've established that you're dramatic. Now that that's out of the way, I was saying... it was so cool how the window was like a portal between two places, and I could see him out there with the colored leaves falling around him like rain. It was the Wood King."

Owen's anger didn't subside. "He's not the Wood King. His *name* is Woodking, Truman Woodking. He was a man and a murderer, the person who stole my brother from me, and now you just *fed* yours to him."

"Here's what I just heard: 'Drama, drama, drama, drama, cry, cry, drama.' Anyway, so the Game Master says, "Touch the window," and I realized that something terrible was going to happen, but I didn't have a chance to stop him. Kinder put his hand on the glass, and it erupted outward into the store–"

"Just like it did when he killed my brother."

"Hel*lo*... I was *talking*. So, your buddy Truman reaches through the window, grabs my brother and rips him right out of reality, pulling him through the window into the forest. Then the window and Kinder were both gone, just like that, and all that was left were the fragments of broken glass on the ground and my hysterical parents."

Owen's eyes went wide. "Your parents were there?!"

"Yeah...so?"

"So they're gonna think I kidnapped you! They already lost one child. God, kid, they're probably losing their minds right now."

She rolled her eyes again. "Yeah... no. They didn't notice I was gone the whole time. I'm pretty sure they're scared of me."

"I can't imagine why."

"Jerk."

"Where is your brother again?"

She huffed. "Listen, I'm pretty sure he's still alive because I watched TikTok videos and Instagram reels of Truman coming through the window at other stores. He killed those people right then and there, but he didn't chop Kinder's head off like the others. He *took* him."

Owen looked like she slapped him in the face. He dug in his pocket for his phone, and the car swerved out of the lane and back. "Hey!" Flower scolded.

"Sorry." He pressed some buttons on his phone and then placed it into the holder on his dashboard.

"It's me, what's up?" a female voice said on the other end.

"Hey, Nina," Owen said. He looked at Flower and put a finger to his lips. She just looked at him, so he assumed that meant she understood. "Sorry to bother you, but do you know if there are any other stores where the victims were abducted, not killed?"

They waited for her to finish coughing, and Flower looked really annoyed by it. Then Nina said, "I actually just got off the phone with Mikey about that. There have been five abductions, all kids around the same ages and demographics as the original five. I don't think it's a coincidence. It's happening again; only this time, he's claiming even more innocent lives. Anyone who presses that button and isn't a necessary part of his recreation ritual is losing their head right in the middle of a Ghostly Halloween superstore."

Owen sighed. "That's what I was afraid of. Alright, I'll let you rest. I'll report back when I know something more. Thanks, Nina."

When he ended the call, Flower said, "My brother is definitely Cody. He was the final boy. That means he's still alive out there. We have to get to him. What do we do?"

"How do you know about Cody?"

"I told you I did my homework. What do we do? How do we get him back?"

"Why are you so worried about him now, after you knew what would happen? No way you watched those videos of the other stores after he went missing. I know you lied because you didn't want me to know just how wicked you are. You knew Truman would come through that window."

"Fine. So I knew. That's the past, old news. Now I need to get Kinder back."

"Feeling guilty?"

She took in a deep breath and blew it out slowly, like she was trying to get every candle on a cake. "No, idiot. I need him. He's the only one who likes me and is nice to me. He's all I've got."

"You probably should have thought about that before you sacrificed him to an undead maniac."

"You probably should have thought about that hair before you put it on your already stupid face, but you didn't, did you?"

"You really are a lovely girl," he said sarcastically.

"You really are a lovely girl," she mocked in an exaggerated caricature of his voice. "So where are we going?"

"To the woods, the old Woodking estate. If your brother's anywhere, it's there."

"Fun," she said, with a genuine smile, her eyes lighting up.

CHAPTER TWELVE
AND THEN THERE WERE MORE

Kinder was running with everything he had. He looked back to see if the Wood King was still following at his creepily leisurely pace. When he did, something collided with him from the right, and he hit the ground hard. His nerves went haywire. This was why Truman wasn't nervous or rushing. Sooner or later, his prey would make a mistake, and he would have them in his enormous hands. *What the heck did I even hit?*

Kinder looked up and found himself staring into the eyes of another boy, just a couple of years older than him by the looks of it. The boy had his hand extended. Kinder seized it and as he was tugged to his feet, the stranger said, "I'm so sorry. I was panicked. He's chasing me. He never stops chasing me. No matter how much I run, he's there every time I turn around."

"Until he isn't," Kinder said upon realizing the Wood King had vanished.

The older boy nodded, his eyes wide with wild fear. "Yeah, but he'll be back. He always comes back. It's like poof—gone—poof—back."

"I know. It means another window opened. He is automatically sent to the new window, and once they're dead, he goes back to where he was before the window appeared."

The new boy shook his head. "But wait...if he was always going back to you, then how could he also be behind me?" He started hyperventilating. "It doesn't make any sense."

Kinder sighed. "It's because this place isn't real. It's some kind of magical afterlife created by the Wizard of the Woods to set things right."

"WHAAT?!!" the new boy screamed.

"Nevvermind. Just keep moving."

The boy took his hand and started running. "Okay. Come on. I saw a place we could hide."

"Wait! Where are we going?" Kinder bellowed as he was dragged through the shower of endlessly falling leaves.

"I saw a house in the distance. It's what I've been running toward this whole time. There's nothing else. Everywhere you look, it's just trees and these stupid leaves." He reached up and swatted them away as they fell toward his head. "The house is our only chance. We have to be close now."

"No, wait!" Kinder cried. "Stop!" But the older boy wouldn't be deterred. He just kept on running and pulling Kinder along with him.

"The house...." Kinder said as he was tugged left and right to avoid hitting trees. "Is it black? Does it lean more to one side?"

"Yeah, that's the one. You've seen it too?"

Kinder dug his heels into the dirt, forcing the other boy to a stop. They almost fell over. The boy glared at him angrily. "What the heck? Do you want to die?"

"No! That's the point!" Kinder yelled. "That's the Wood King's house!"

"What?" the boy asked quietly, sounding defeated. "Oh no. Oh, come on. No."

"Crap," Kinder said, looking past the boy. "It's too late. We're already here."

"What?" the boy said again. He turned around and looked. Kinder stood beside him, staring as well. The giant jet black house loomed over them like a shadow cast by death.

"I think no matter where we ran, we were always going to end up here," Kinder told him, sounding defeated. The boy looked at him with wet eyes.

"Just like he never stopped following all of us, we were all running the same route to the same place, but separately."

"Yeah." Kinder's eyes widened. "Hey, wait....you said all of us. You know where the others are?"

The boy swallowed hard. Tears left his eyes and ran down his olive cheeks. "Were. One boy wasn't fast enough. As soon as he came through the window, he was scared frozen. I watched it from behind a tree. I was trying to wave him on, but didn't move a muscle. He just stared at the Wood King and peed his pants. It was so messed up, man. I came out of hiding, waving my arms and yelling and… and…."

"Truman took his head, didn't he?"

"It hit me. I was running toward him, and it flew off and hit me." The boy was sobbing hard. "Then I'm screaming and staring into that monster's horrible mask. I'm pretty sure it was the barbarian guy from Game of Thrones, except like set on fire or something. It was horrible. I ran, and he turned ever so slowly and just followed like he knew I couldn't escape."

"Looked more like Aquaman to me, but yeah." Kinder exhaled and looked back nervously. Truman still hadn't returned. For some reason, that made him more nervous. "I know. It doesn't give much hope, but the wizard said one had already died. He said there were five of us all together. That means there should still be two people somewhere."

"What wizard??"

Kinder shook his head. "It doesn't matter. We have to find the other two, or this will never end. One of us has to live for it to end, even if it's Truman Woodking."

"What?"

Kinder wanted to slap the other boy. "Focus, okay? Did you see anyone else?"

The boy swallowed. He nodded. "I was stunned after that other boy's head bounced off my face. The Wood King and his oozing barbarian mask were coming. A girl appeared out of nowhere and grabbed my arm. She dragged me in this direction. I lost track of her at some point, but I didn't see him get her."

Kinder thought for a moment. "No matter where in the country we come from, once we get on the path toward the house, our paths converge. She had already been here running. She had to be. If she hadn't, he would have appeared at her window, but he was at that other boy's window, and she was able to run to you."

"So where the heck did she go?"

Kinder turned and pointed at the house.

The other boy swallowed again. "Well, if we're supposed to be like the original kids, the last person has to be another boy. So where is he?"

Kinder turned around and pointed again. Another boy was barreling toward them, pumping his arms as hard as he could. "Stop!" the boy with Kinder yelled.

The newcomer tried to hit the brakes but couldn't stop and ran into him. Kinder reached down and helped them both up. "I'm Kinder," he said, "in case one of us makes it out and the others don't, we should know each other's names so we can tell someone."

"Gary," said the new boy.

"Petey," said the boy who had been running with Kinder. "The girl who's probably already at the house is named Adley."

"More importantly," Gary said, looking back. "Where is the Wood King, and why isn't he following us?"

Kinder pointed at the towering black house that bent toward them like an ocean wave. "This time... he's waiting for us."

"We should just not go," said Petey. "We should run. We just turn around. Come on."

Kinder sighed. "You know it won't do any good. All the running we did just led us here because it's where we're supposed to be."

"I don't like it," Gary said, "but I think he's right. So any plans?"

Kinder stared at that awful house. It looked like the mouth of a monster ready to swallow him whole. He took a deep breath and said, "Yeah. Stay away from the windows."

CHAPTER THIRTEEN
WE'RE HERE

The car stopped at the entrance to the woods, and Flower was amazed by how frightened she suddenly felt. "So... uh....this is it, huh?"

"This is it," Owen said, getting out of the car. "Maybe you should wait here, stay hidden."

She shook her head. "No way. I'm coming with you."

He frowned but didn't argue. "Then come on. I think I still know the way, even after all these years."

"You walked it looking for your brother?"

He nodded. "We all did. The whole community was out here searching for those kids. Police wished different once we found 'em."

Flower nodded. "Alright then, lead the way."

He eyed her suspiciously but started walking. She knew he was wary of her, like everyone was, like everyone should have been if she were being honest with herself. She didn't have any intention of throwing him into anything, though, at least not at this moment. If it came down to it, and she could save herself or save her brother, she would kick this guy into Truman's blade in a heartbeat. It annoyed her that he knew it.

"It's this way," he said, looking back to make sure she was following. "It's kind of creepy how it hasn't changed at all. The grass that was trampled by our feet that day never grew out again. It's still crushed into a path. Look."

Flower did look and he was right. Part of her was absolutely terrified, and part of her was entirely fascinated. "So you think they're really here? Like in these woods?" she asked as he rounded a tree and gasped for a second when she lost sight of him. She sighed when she found him again and hurried to catch up. "I mean, what if they're here but not here? That's what HOrrOrGrrrrl42137 on TikTok said."

"What did they say?"

"That they're taken to the woods, but if you go to the woods, you'll never find them because they're not actually in this dimension or reality or whatever."

"And you believe that?" He swatted tall grass to the side and stepped through to find the path continued on the other side.

Flower jumped through the tall greenery without moving it. She stumbled over a tree root but caught herself and rushed after him. Crows burst from the trees and launched skyward. "I don't know. I guess anything is possible," she said when she caught up."

"Yeah," he answered. She had expected an argument and was surprised to find none. When they broke through the trees to stand before the giant black house, she shuddered. It wasn't quite jet black anymore as age had its way with the wood, but it was black in places and charcoal gray in others, faded white in some, and just plain wood grain in other bits. It was no less menacing, though. In fact, the leaning looked worse, like if they went inside and went to the rooms on the right, the whole house might collapse with them in it.

"So you think they're in there?" she asked him.

Owen stared at the house for a minute before answering. "I don't know," he told her. "I don't understand any of this, but I don't have any better ideas. I just want it all to be over."

"I know you're a liar too," she said. He pulled his eyes from the house to turn and look at her.

"Excuse me?"

"You told me you had a kid, but I heard you tell that cop that you had a wife and a dog."

He raised his brows. "Well, you may not understand this, but the way I see it....that dog is my son. I love him with my whole heart."

"And you're the guy that's going to save the day? The human with dog children? God help me."

"Shut it," he said. He lifted his shirt and showed her the gun holstered at his waistband. "My odds are better than yours. You wouldn't have even gotten here without me. Don't bite the hand that feeds."

"Ugh. You are so corny. I'm glad your dog child doesn't understand how annoying dad jokes are."

"Whatever. Just be quiet and keep your eyes peeled."

"My eyes *are* peeled," she told him. "That's why I saw the old man spying on us."

"What? Where?" he asked with sudden alarm.

Flower looked toward where she had just seen the man peeking around a tree, but she lost track of him. She chewed on her lip. "He was right over there," she said, pointing. "Is he part of this?"

"I don't know," Owen said with a nervous frown. "Let's just move. I want to get this over with and get out of here."

"There's a lot you don't know, huh?" Flower asked with annoyance.

"Yes, I'm not ashamed to admit it. I have no idea what we're about to walk into."

"Fantastic."

He stopped and looked at her, but she was looking past him at the trees, searching for some sign of the strange old man she had seen. "Oh, and you do?" he asked.

"I know more than *you*," she said snidely.

"Like what?"

"I thought you were in a hurry and wanted to get home."

"Yeah, that's what I thought." He turned back and marched his way up to the front door of the looming house. The sky grew dark almost instantly. There was a crack of thunder, and rain began to pour down onto them. "Oh, what the hell?"

"Are you afraid of rain now, too?" Flower asked, coming up behind him.

"I'm afraid of a thousand-dollar suit getting ruined, yeah."

Flower laughed and shook her head. "You wore a thousand-dollar suit to go traipse through the woods, oh, wise man."

He growled through his teeth and looked ready to punch her, which only made her laugh more. He grabbed the doorknob and tried to turn it. "Dang. It's locked."

Lightning flashed, illuminating the house. A shadow passed by one of the windows on the inside. Flower cried out, but then she said, "Someone is in there."

"Well, the door is locked. We'll have to find another way."

"Just break a window," she told him. "Or are you afraid of what might happen?"

He looked at her crooked grin and made a face like he wondered what kind of evil he brought with him into these woods. She knew that face. She had seen it so many times, even on her own parents. It only widened her smile.

"Maybe there's a back door," he said, walking around the large, ominously black house. Behind him, Flower laughed loudly.

CHAPTER FOURTEEN
THE BEGINNING OF THE END

The three boys crept toward the house. They were on high alert, huddling close together and looking around nervously for signs of danger. Suddenly, all sound was gone like they were in a vacuum. No birds flew or squawked, no wind ripped through. Even the leaves stopped falling. They froze before the house and watched the last ones touch down, drifting ever so slowly toward the pile at their feet.

"What the heck is happening?" Petey asked in a whisper.

"The end of the story," said Kinder, "for bad or for worse."

"How 'bout for good?" asked Gary. "Let's not be fatalistic. We're not dead yet."

"I know who you are," Kinder said. "You're Cole."

"How do you know so much about this stuff?" Petey asked.

Kinder frowned. "My sister.... Has some dark interests."

They were looking not just for Truman but for any sign of where Adley was. "Maybe she's not here," Petey said worriedly. "Maybe you're wrong."

Kinder shook his head. "I'm not. This is where all of our paths lead, hers too, I know it."

"Adley," Gary called in a loud whisper. Kinder noticed a shadow move past one of the windows. He jumped. Petey must have seen it too because he latched onto Kinder's arm. "Adley!"

"Over here," Adley called back. She was crouched behind a rusted pickup truck sitting on its rims. Kinder knew it from the stories Flower read obsessively. He didn't know about the animatronic or how the story ended, just the true crime stuff. She loved to share it with him because she knew it scared him. It was Truman's old truck. He must have left it there and followed Cody on foot before getting gunned down. It just sat there and died like its owner.

They moved over toward where she was hiding so the group could be together like they were meant to be. "Watch out for the windows," she said. "He's using the windows. I think he has a gun."

"Fantastic," Gary said as they hurried toward her through the sea of wet leaves. It wasn't lost on Kinder that even their hurried, pounding steps made no sound. They reached the truck and Kinder ducked down beside Adley. Sound returned with the crack of a gun shot. It was the loudest thing Kinder had ever heard. His eyes went wide and his mouth fell open as Petey went down. As he fell, he grabbed for Gary, and took him down with him. Kinder couldn't help but think it was good. If Gary was still standing, he might have been shot too.

Kinder crawled on his hands and knees over to Petey to see if he was alright. There was a hole in his forehead and his eyes were staring blankly. "Get him off me!" Gary cried.

Adley rushed over and pulled the dead boy off of him. Kinder just backed out of the way until he hit the truck, staring in shock. The exit wound was far worse and poor Gary was coated in Petey. "Still feeling optimistic?" Kinder couldn't help but ask the boy, who glared at him through the chunky red paint.

"What are we gonna do?" Adley asked, her breaths quick. Kinder could see how hard her heart was beating with the movement of her shirt.

He tried to remember the pictures from Flower's articles. His head turned left and right and he said, "I think the Ghostly Halloween store is through the woods that way. That's where it ended last time."

She nodded. "Screw it," she said. "Let's do this." Adley stood and bolted for the trees. There was a whistling and the boys watched in horror as an arrow hit the back of her neck and stuck her to the tree. "Help," she called. "I- I think I'm paralyzed. I-I can't move my arms or legs to try to get free. Don't leave me like this. Please."

The boys looked at each other but neither moved. They were too afraid the same thing would happen to them. Adley started screaming then. Kinder cringed.

"Anymore bright ideas," the blood-coated boy beside him asked. Kinder said nothing. He had nothing to say.

CHAPTER FIFTEEN
THE WAY IN

Owen threw his shoulder into the door until it came flying open and he fell into the nightmare house. He looked back at Flower. "Ha. To hell with the windows."

She shrugged and stepped over him, walking fearlessly through the dust and cobwebs. She went room to room, cringing at the disgusting remains of food that had rotted for so many years and the rats that looked for something they were willing to still nibble on. "No one has been in here for so long, but I saw someone moving around inside."

"Like you saw the old man in the trees. I think you're not really right in the head, girl."

"My name is Flower and I'm just fine. I just think we're missing something. I saw someone moving within but I saw them through the window. When we actually came in, the house was empty. Maybe what I saw through the window was the same world the window led to in the Ghostly Halloween store?"

"You and the dang windows," Owen said as he went upstairs. Flower stepped up onto the lower steps but didn't go further. She looked up and waited for him to conduct his search.

When he returned, she said, "Anything?"

"No."

"Still think I'm wrong?"

"No, yes, I don't know…. I mean, what are we supposed to do even if it is the windows?"

"Go through them," Flower said matter-of-factly. She ran and jumped, throwing her arms in front of her face to shield herself. Then she crashed through the window with a screaming shatter of glass.

Owen's eyes went wide. He could already imagine the girl's parents screaming at him. He hurried down the steps, across the wooden floor to the window, and looked out. He saw nothing. "Flower," he called, quietly at first. Then louder, "Flower!"

There was no response. He ran back to the door and hurried through it around to where she would have come out. She wasn't there and there was no sign that she ever was, just broken glass like the windows left in the store. Owen roared with frustration. He bit his lip, and took his gun out. Then he went into the house and stared at the window on the other side of the door. Did it work for all of them? Did they all lead to the same place or would he end up somewhere else?

He stared at the gun in his hand. "Just go. You can do this. Come on. There's kids counting on you." He took a deep breath and when he let it out, he didn't give himself a chance to think or change his mind. He just ran as hard and fast as he could and dove through the glass window with a crash.

CHAPTER SIXTEEN
DEATH COMES CALLING

Kinder didn't know what to do. He was frozen, petrified, sure he was going to die. He looked over at Adley hanging by the arrow through her neck. She'd stopped calling to them. He didn't know if she gave up or just died. Ocassionally, gunfire would pepper the old truck to let them know that Truman was still there, watching from the windows of the black house.

"There's no way out," he said when he finally spoke. "The wizard said it didn't matter if Truman was the one to live. We're going to die."

Gary wiped his eyes so he could see better. He was still wearing Petey. "What if we do what no one did?"

"Huh?"

"Fight, man. What if we bum rush that stupid house and ninja kick the crap out of that bully?"

Kinder shook his head. "There's no way. He's huge...and armed."

"And we outnumber him, bruh. We go together. It's better than sitting here waiting for death, isn't it?"

Kinder didn't like it, but he didn't like any of this. He couldn't think of anything better. With a sigh, he nodded. "On three."

Gary and him both stood but remained hunched to stay behind cover. Gary met his eyes and nodded. "1...2...now!"

Together they ran around the truck and sprinted toward the front door of the house. There was no gunfire or flying arrows and Kinder's confidence waned even as the battle cry emerged from his lips. They reached the door and a huge hand crashed through the window to the right. It seized Gary by the top of his head, palming it like a basketball. Kinder cried out and fell backwards onto his rump. He looked up as Gary kicked and punched at the massive man and his muscled arm that remained latched to the boy's head. Kinder knew he should get up, he should fight, he should do something, but he couldn't. He wondered what Cody felt like in this moment, when he realized he was the last one. Was he able to move? Was he scared? Did he fight?

A second massive hand came through the now glassless window and clamped down on the kicking Gary's shoulder. That hand pressed down as the other lifted up and right before Kinder's eyes, Gary's head was literally torn form his neck, blood splashing in every direction. Kinder found the ability to move and crab walked backward to avoid the red tide splashing down at him. Gary's head landed between his feet, staring up at him with a look of horror. "I'm sorry, I'm sorry, I'm sorry," Kinder chanted as he continued to scrambled backward on the ground.

The Wood King dropped Gary's body in a crumpled heap and forced his own massive body through the window, his mask's stiff hair catching and tearing on the shards of remaining glass. Kinder looked up and waited for the end.

CHAPTER SEVENTEEN
RESCUE?

P op! Pop! Pop! Kinder heard the sounds before he realized what they were. When he opened his eyes, Truman Woodking and his drooping tan skinned mask was stumbling backward. Someone grabbed the back of his collar and tugged him to his feet. He had no idea what was happening. Then he saw a cool guy in a beautiful suit, with shades and a lavender gun that sparkled like glitter facing off with the monster who had been about to murder him. Kinder turned to see who had his collar and found himself looking into Flower's eyes. She smiled at him.

"Now's the time when we run," she said.

"But what about him?" Kinder said pointing back at the newcomer.

"That's Owen. He's been waiting a long time for this and he has a gun. Let's go," Flower told him. Kinder nodded and ran with her into and through the trees. They felt closer together than before and the branches whipped and tore at him as he ran.

"I don't know what's gonna happen," he said as his sister pulled him along. "The Wizard of the Woods recreated the original event for finality, to find closure, but there were already five of us and the girl died already. You and Owen aren't supposed to be here."

"Like always, little brother, I'm the wild card."

They reached the end of the woods and saw the road they had to cross to get to the Ghostly Halloween Superstore but they couldn't go any further. It was like they hit an invisible wall. "What's happening?" Flower snapped angrily.

Kinder shook his head and backed up. "It's wrong. It's wrong and now we're all gonna die."

Flower slapped the crap out of him and he stared at her, his eyes bugging out of his head. "Stop it," she commanded. "It won't let us go further because this isn't the real world. This version of that world only goes this far. It's a recreation. All of it. We need to find a window to get back."

Behind them they heard more gunfire and things crashing and breaking. Kinder shook his head again. "Then we still lose. The windows were to find five people who fit. The ones who didn't were killed instantly but the five of us were found and mostly disposed of already. There's no reason for another window to open.

Flower chewed on her lip and looked around. "There has to be one, just one."

Kinder had tears running from his eyes. "There's not. I'm telling you, it's over."

"And I told you to shut up. We have to go back."

"What?" Kinder asked, his face mirroring the terror in his voice. "No. We can't go back."

Flower rolled her eyes. Well, we can't go this way. Do you want to live or not?"

"Yes, but–"

"But nothing. We got here because we came through windows in that damn evil house. That means we can take windows back. There's still windows on the second floor."

"If it doesn't work, the fall will kill us," Kinder cried.

"Then you better hope it works." She grabbed his hand and ran back through the woods.

CHAPTER EIGHTEEN
THE END

When they broke through the trees back near the house, Kinder couldn't help but stop beside Adley to feel for a pulse. She was gone. He frowned but deep down he felt it was better than her hanging there, suffering.

Owen and Truman were engaged and wrestling. Truman had Owen by the wrist so he couldn't fire his weapon. Owen was kicking at him trying to get him to let go. "We have to help him," Kinder cried out.

Flower huffed. "Why? So his dog doesn't lose his daddy? No. He's got Truman occupied. We have to help ourselves."

"It's not right."

"I don't care if it's right or wrong, it's survival. Now, go."

Flower shoved Kinder before her and they ran for the open front door of the leaning house. As they ran through their heads turned to look at Owen. His eyes met theirs and widened as the Wood King's giant hand plunged right through his belly.

Kinder froze in the doorway. "There's no time," Flower commanded, but he couldn't go. He held Owen's gaze as Truman Woodking ripped his insides from his body and tossed them in the air like confetti.

"Come the heck on!" Flower shouted, but Kinder couldn't move until Owen hit the ground, his life gone to wherever it went from there.

Finally, Kinder moved when Flower tugged him toward the stairs. He still looked back to see the Wood King walking leisurely toward them, his hand dripping gore. "He's not even using his weapons," Kinder said as his sister pulled him up the stairs toward the second floor of the house. "He's literally tearing us apart with his bare hands."

"All the more reason to run," Flower told him.

Kinder looked back and the massive man was in the doorway of the house staring up the stairs at them through the warped eyeholes of his melted barbarian mask. They hit the landing as he hit the bottom of the staircase. They ran down the hall as he pounded his way up after them, each footfall echoing through the old house like a crash of thunder.

Flower didn't even say anything. She just pulled her brother with her by the hand and dove through the bedroom window. They screamed when they hit the open air and realized how high up they were. Kinder turned his head to look back and saw that horrible mask at the window watching them.

Then they hit the ground and were still screaming until they realized they weren't dead and had no broken limbs.

They looked at each other. Everything was dark, but the floor beneath them was solid, tiled, not dirt and grass. They both looked away from each other to survey their surroundings and saw powered down animatronics and peg walls of masks and capes. They were back in Ghostly Halloween but it looked long closed. "I guess they gave up on finding me," Kinder said quietly.

"They never cared to find me in the first place," Flower answered with a shrug.

"Is it over?" Kinder asked. He put his hand out to push himself to his feet and groaned as broken glass cut his palm.

"It's all over the ground," Flower said. She grabbed the game master's tattered robe to pull herself up. Kinder looked at her and saw what she held and he stumbled backward, falling back to the ground. "Relax," she told him.

"It-it's him," he said, pointing at the animatronic.

Flower laughed. "Yeah but he stopped working right after you went through the window. Look." She stomped on his pedal and nothing happened. "The whole place is shut down and closed for the night anyway. It's dark as hell."

Kinder swallowed but he got to his feet. "We have to find Mom and Dad."

Flower rolled her eyes at the sentiment. "Yeah, I guess. I'm sure they're super broken up."

He frowned at her. Then there was a bright light from behind her that cut through the darkness of the closed store. A massive hand grabbed flower by the hair and lifted her off the ground. "No!" Kinder screamed.

He didn't hesitate. He was scared of a lot, almost everything, but he and his sister stuck together. He dove on the madman's giant back and reached around to stick his fingers through the eye holes of the mask and the eyes behind them. Truman Woodking roared in agony and threw Flower across the room. She flew into the tunnel of mirrors and disappeared. Kinder hoped she was alright. Truman was stomping around trying to fling him off but he held tight. He saw Flower's legs sticking out of the curtained hall and they weren't moving. He felt terror worse than he had felt even when he was in the woods. Kinder felt like Flower was his responsibility. She was different, dark, dangerous, but she was his. No one understood her or treated her with love or kindness. They all just wanted her gone. Even though he was technically younger, Kinder took care of her. If she died, he would never forgive himself.

Truman reached back and grabbed a firm hold of him. "Uh oh," Kinder said as the man physically tore him free from his back. Kinder reached out and grabbed the mask as he was ripped away. It came off in his hands, and when he hit the ground painfully, he groaned and looked up at Truman's true face.

It was far more melted than the mask he wore. His nose was little more than a slit in his skull. His lips were all but gone and his teeth were yellowed and jutting in different directions. His eyes were now bleeding from Kinder's fingers and added to the horror. Stray hairs shot in clumps from his mottled skull. His ears were just fleshy mounds melted to his head. One cheek was gone and when he turned, Kinder could see the teeth and gums through the hole.

Suddenly, Kinder felt sad. He looked up at this monster and realized Truman was probably just like his sister. He was probably seen as evil and monstrous, bullied and harassed, ignored and unloved. He just wanted to be left alone and kids broke into his house and messed with his things. He was just trying to protect himself. Somewhere in there was a boy who wanted to be loved.

Kinder got to his feet and stared at the giant deformed man. He opened his mouth to tell Truman he was sorry when there was a series of thunderclaps. Truman's deformed head burst like a water balloon thrown at a wall.

His giant body fell and a tide of blood and brains washed across the floor to Kinder's feet.

Where the giant had stood, was a police officer. "You kids alright? I just couldn't bring myself to go home. I felt like you would come back at some point and need help. I know the store was closed and I'm probably gonna catch flack for this, but I'm also glad I was here."

Kinder couldn't speak. He was thinking of someone shooting his sister and thinking they saved the day because they rid the world of something they didn't understand.

"Mikey?" a voice groaned. "Officer Mikey?"

"Do I know you? The cop said. He shone his flashlight in the direction of the voice. A groggy Flower was stumbling toward him.

"Not really I guess," she said. "But I know you. Owen... he's dead. You should tell his dog."

The cop sighed. "Damn."

She looked at Kinder then. "I just figured it out. His mask. It was the Trashman from that kid's movie."

EPILOGUE
HOUSE CALL

Kinder and Flower's Dad opened the front door to the house. He stared at the old man on the stoop. "Can I help you with something?"

The old man smiled. "No. I believe it's the other way around. I can help you."

The dad eyed the old man warily as his wife walked over to ask what was happening. "I'm not sure," he said honestly.

"I know what your daughter is," the old man said. "She's a monster, just like Truman Woodking and Martin who folks like to call the Death Digger. Soon she will move up from animals and your boy will stick with her no matter what. You will both have to live with the things they do together, the lives lost."

"That's not fact," the kids' father said angrily. "Who are you? How dare you come to our home to make accusations about our kids!"

"I think it is," his wife said to him with a hint of sadness. "Come on. You know it too."

The old man smiled. "I am here to offer you a solution. I have a place I can bring them, a place where they will not be able to hurt anyone and they will have everything they need. It's a house in the middle of nowhere out in my woods. They will be safe so you need not have guilt and more importantly, the world will be safe from them."

"What woods are yours?" asked the father.

"All of them."

"You're him," the mother said. "You're real. The Wizard of the Woods."

His smile widened. "At your service."

"This house," she said. "Tell us more."

Her husband shook his head. "No. What? Why are we entertaining this? This is crazy."

The old man nodded and smiled again. "It's fully furnished but each of the things inside it is just like your children, things that were dangerous to remain where they were. Now they are all safe in the house together. It's a house of abandoned things if you will."

"I don't want to add our children to that, to abandon them," the fathers growled, his glare directed at his wife, not the stranger on their doorstep.

"But they'll be safe," she said. "They can live without hurting anyone. Can you live with it if they kill?"

"They won't!"

"They will," the old man said without his smile faltering. "At least.... she will, and he will aid her. He'll protect her, help her clean up, dispose of the body. He'll do whatever it takes to keep her safe. They may bicker but they have a bond that runs deep. You must believe me or rue the day when I'm proven correct. Those are the only choices."

"I want no part of this," the father said, storming off.

The mother sighed. She looked sad but she nodded at the old man. "Can you just take Flower? Kinder will be a good boy away from her. I know he will."

The old man sighed too. "On the contrary, he will stop at nothing to find her and bring her home. It will ruin his life."

She wiped tears from her eyes and sniffled. She hated to admit it but she knew he was right. How did it come to this? How did her babies end up so wrong?

As if sensing her question, the wizard said, "Some people are just born bad—-even with us. We are all meant to be indifferent, to serve a purpose and be neither good nor bad, but the Sorcerer is just evil. He always was and always will be and we cannot change it or stop it. This is your girl, Flower. On the other hand, the Witch's love for her son has led her astray and taken her down a dark path. Don't let that be you."

The mother covered her mouth, and her tears came with force, though she kept them quiet. She nodded. "Take them quickly before I cave and change my mind. They're upstairs sleeping. Don't let me see it."

"You'll see nothing. Mortals only see what I want them to." The old man moved past her into the house. He ascended the stairs but never came back down. She turned and looked up the stairwell but all she saw was darkness. Frowning, she climbed the stairs. She opened the kids' rooms one at a time. They were both gone, their beds unmade and sheets tossed aside. The mother walked to the window and looked out at the night, but all she saw was trees.

END FOR NOW

Find out what happens to Kinder and Flower next in the upcoming...
House of Abandoned Things
By Boe Healy

SOme places are JUST bad.
The House of Abandoned Things
BOE HEALY

CHAPTER ONE

THE HOUSE FROM NOWHERE

Kinder blinked. He had no idea where he was or how he had gotten there, and looking around didn't help. There was a whole lot of nothing in every direction: just grass, dirt, and dead trees. It was all so green, not just the grass but also the trees and the overabundance of hovering clouds as well. Even the sky was a shade of green. It didn't seem like it could be real. The whole place looked sick, and he couldn't help but wonder if he were dreaming. Could a place be sick?

He felt someone beside him and turned. His sister, Flower, was there looking just as lost as he was. "What the hell is this place?" she asked with annoyance.

Kinder smirked, thinking of how their parents would have scowled if they heard her say 'hell.' "No idea. Look at the clouds. You ever see anything like that?"

"I see a witch on a broom. Up there. That one." She pointed.

"Oh yeah. I see it," he said with a giggle. "I meant the green."

"Oh, yeah. No. That's weird. You think we're dreaming?"

"Well, I did, but then you showed up, Flower. How could we both be dreaming the same thing... together?

"Hmm..." she said thoughtfully. She looked down at her foot as she kicked an algae-green rock. "But like... what if one of us isn't real and they're just like part of the dream?"

Kinder scrunched his face and chewed his lip. "Well, it would have to be you coz I was here first."

"Nuh uh," Flower said, scowling just like their mom did whenever they said bad words. "I was just back there." She gestured with her thumb over her shoulder. "I was watching you looking around like you were dumb."

"I'm not dumb, Flower. We're lost."

"I'm not dumb either, butthole, so I didn't need you to tell me that."

Kinder frowned. He kicked dirt. "In school, they said when a man tells a woman something she already knows, it's called mansplaining."

Flower just stared at him with a dumbfounded look on her face. She sighed. "Well, you're not a man; you're a kid, so quit kidsplaining."

"I'm not doing it on purpose, you jerk!"

"Jerk," she mimicked. "You definitely use kid words. It makes you seem little."

"I'm *not* little. I'm taller than you. I'm almost five feet tall."

"I don't care. You're still the little brother. It doesn't matter how tall you get."

"You're eleven months older than me. That's not even a full year."

"Kidsplaining. Look out there."

Kinder followed where his sister was pointing. He still had to squint. Whatever it was, it was far. It just looked like an amorphous dark green blob to him. "What?"

"Well, I don't know, Kinder, but it's something. Look around at all the nothing. If there's something that way, shouldn't we *go* that way?"

He chewed his lip and looked back over his shoulder. There was nothing but an eternal expanse of green. "But how did we get here, Flower? What if we walk far from the exit and the way back home? I'm scared."

His sister laughed at him. She walked over and physically turned him. Then she waved her arm about. She was scowling like their mom again. "Do you *see* an exit?" she asked angrily. "Is there a doorway home in all that grass? Do you see a creepy van that our kidnappers dropped us off in? Because me? I see frickin' grass."

"You overdo the bad words," he said with a pout, looking away from her steely gaze. "Makes you seem like a try-hard, like you're just trying to be cool."

"No. I'm just not a baby, little brother."

"You really think we've been kidnapped? At least there's no windows. I'd be happy to never see another one again."

He saw the anger fade from her face. She sighed and looked away. "I don't know," she said quietly. "Someone did something. We didn't just wander off and wind up here. This place can't even be near us. North Carolina is all grey, orange, and brown; it's not green. It's the mountains. Do you see any mountains?"

"So... what? Someone drugged us, drove us, or flew us somewhere far away and then just let us out and *left*?"

"I don't know!" she snapped. She whirled around and started tramping through the grass. "You want to stay here? Go ahead. I'm going to see what's out there."

Kinder chewed on his finger as he watched her go. Then he yelled, "Wait!" and ran to catch up. When he was beside her, trying hard to match her gait, he said, "Do you think there's cameras somewhere and they're watching us? If they were in the grass, we wouldn't know."

"I don't know."

"Do you think there's something or someone else out here with us?"

"I don't know."

"What if it's someone bad? Someone dangerous? And that's why they left?"

"I. Don't. Know. Kinder."

"Well, it doesn't make sense that they would just take us out here and leave us here. And where the hell even is here?"

Flower smirked at her brother's use of the word 'hell.' "I don't frickin' know," she said back.

"What if we're stuck here forever?"

"Then they better have Twinkies. I don't want to live in a world without Twinkies."

Kinder looked around nervously as they tromped through the grass together. "I don't think they have *anything*."

"They'd better."

"Or else what?"

"You know or else what."

"If they do have 'em, I bet they're green."

"As long as they taste the same, I don't give a crap."

They didn't speak after that. They just kept walking. Even with the cloud cover, it managed to be hot. Neither said it, but both wondered if the sun would be green when they finally saw it.

They continued toward the thing in the distance despite not knowing what it was. They just needed a destination—direction—something. After what felt like forever, they were close enough to finally see it clearly. Kinder was the first one to say it.

"It's a house."

"I can see that," Flower growled, glaring at him. "Maybe they have Twinkies."

"What if it's where the bad people live?"

"We don't even know there *are* bad people, Kinder."

"Well, someone brought us here. Do you think Mom and Dad abandoned us?"

"They wouldn't dare."

"I don't like it."

"Then stay outside." Kinder watched as his sister approached the front door of the house. He swallowed nervously, and it hurt because his throat was dry. He wished he had some spicy juice (That's what he called flavored, carbonated water) like his dad always gave him.

The house was as green as everything, and strangely, the old wood didn't seem painted. It wasn't flaking at all or chipped anywhere. It was just... green. Like the wood was naturally green, just like everything else in this place. Kinder didn't like it one bit. He cringed when his sister didn't even knock and went straight for the doorknob.

His cringe intensified when the door opened inward, and Flower glanced back at him with a mischievous grin.

The door didn't creak like the haunted house doors in scary movies, like the ones their dad watched and their mom wanted them kept away from. It didn't make any sound at all. It was completely silent. Kinder thought about it then, and the whole place had been quiet since they got there. There were no animal sounds, no whistling breeze, and no dried grass crunch. Nothing. He was feeling more and more freaked out. He looked down at the grass. It looked lush and healthy. When he looked up, his sister was staring at him with wide eyes.

"Are you gonna come in or stay out here and act like a scared little baby?"

The house scared Kinder, but the idea of being out there alone was far more terrifying. He chewed on his already whittled fingernail, but he walked up to the open front door where she stood impatiently waiting.

As soon as they stepped into the strange green house in the middle of nowhere, the door slammed shut. In the silence, the bang was impossibly loud, and they both yelped. Flower was doubled over laughing, and Kinder was trembling, hugging himself.

When they turned to take in their surroundings, they saw people screaming in terror and agony. Blood sprayed at them, washed over them like a tidal wave. Hands clawed at them for help. They heard blades chopping, meat slicing, and bones snapping.

Then it was over.

Both kids checked themselves and each other for the blood they saw. There wasn't a single drop on either of them. Flower was trembling now, too. They were both panting, gasping for air, their hearts racing. "What the hell was that?" Flower asked.

It was finally Kinder's turn to say, "I don't know."

He tried the door. It was locked and wouldn't budge. When he looked back at his sister with panicked eyes, she said, "Alright. It's okay. Don't freak out. There's windows. If we have to, we'll break out of here."

Kinder reluctantly let go of the doorknob and whirled on her. "Don't freak out. There's windows?" he said, like she'd gone crazy. "There's no safety in windows, Flower!"

"Pssh," she said, waving him off. "I saved your butt because of windows, so whatever." When they stood side by side once more and looked out into the house again, there were no more sounds of horrible butcherings and no shower of blood or deafening screams. They faced an all too ordinary living room with a couch, a TV in an entertainment center, a coffee table, a rocking chair, and a fireplace, flames silently whipping about within. Who lit them? They both wondered. There was a doorway on the other side, and what looked like a kitchen through it. The siblings stood there quietly, not knowing what to do. Something popped in the fireplace, and they jumped.

Flower took a deep breath and huffed. "Well, if they've got Twinkies, they're probably in the kitchen, so that's where I'm going."

Kinder said nothing. He just watched. Flower crossed the living room and passed through a doorway on the other side. "Place is kinda nice in an old-timey kind of way," she said.

He wanted to say, "I don't like it," but knew if he did, she would only tease him. He did like that the contents of the house weren't green like everything else. "What do you see?" he asked.

"What you would expect," she called back. "A bartop counter, fridge, cabinets, oven, dishwasher, sink, and a doorway to the dining room with a table and chairs, a pantry, and a china cabinet. No monsters or dead bodies if that's what you're thinking. No Twinkies either, at least not in these cabinets. Maybe they keep them refrigerated."

Kinder listened as she opened the fridge. Then she screamed, and before he even knew what he was doing, he was rushing across the living room toward her. When he got to the doorway, she didn't look hurt. She did look scared, though—terrified, actually. He'd never seen her like that. "What happened?" he asked, but he could barely hear his own voice.

She just shook her head. "When I... when I touched the fridge handle, it was like before... I saw people screaming and dying and heard them being broken, torn apart... sawed. It was... I can still hear it. Bzzzzzzzzzz." She shook her head again.

Her brother shook his head. He stumbled backward, away from the kitchen, and put his hand down on the top of the rocking chair. As soon as he did, he saw an old woman begging for mercy and reaching for him. A knife came from behind and stabbed her in her bony chest. When the black-gloved hand pulled it back out, blood sprayed toward Kinder. The old woman coughed, and her teeth flew out. He yanked his hand away and looked at it like he'd been burned.

Flower came up beside him. "Something's wrong with this place," she said. Kinder had trouble paying attention. He was staring at the empty rocking chair, wondering how long ago that poor old woman had sat in it. He couldn't help but look down, expecting her teeth to be on the ground at his feet, but there was only green hardwood floor. "I think it will happen whenever we touch certain things."

"Everything," Kinder said. "I hate this place."

"Not everything," Flower told him with a shake of her head. "It didn't happen when I looked in the cabinets, just when I tried to open the fridge."

Kinder thought about that. He chewed on his fingernail again. Then he said, "Hold on. I have an idea."

He didn't like it, and he certainly didn't want to try it, but he couldn't know if he was right until he did, so he walked over to the pantry. He dragged his hands across the walls as he went. The house showed him no visions of death. When he reached the pantry, he held his breath and grabbed the doors. When he opened them, he expected the worst and sighed with relief when nothing came. Flower had followed behind, and he could feel her watching intently, curious as to what he was thinking.

Inside the pantry were bare wooden shelves built into the back wall. The green continued. The only other thing was an old aluminum popcorn tin—not green. Kinder took in a deep breath and held it in, then reached for the tin to open the lid. As soon as he touched it, he saw bloody fingers reach for it and tear it open. They hurriedly dumped the popcorn out all over the floor and dropped a dead cat inside, its head turned unnaturally and eyes bulging. Blood dripped from its open torso into the tin, sounding like rain as it hit. Ping. Ping. Ping. Ping.

Kinder pulled his hand away. "It happened again, didn't it?" Flower asked from behind him.

He turned to look at her and nodded when their eyes met. "But not when I opened the pantry, only when I touched the popcorn tin. The green things are actually the safe things."

Flower's eyes lit up. "The cabinets and the pantry—they're built in. It's not the house, just the things inside of it."

Her brother nodded again.

"I take it back. You're not an idiot," she said.

"You didn't say I was an idiot," he responded, looking offended.

"Out loud," she said with a laugh.

"This house is full of evil things, Flower. We need to go."

"We should touch something together," she said. He winced when she sounded excited. "Come on, little brother. I think everything in this house has its own story. Maybe they're connected somehow. Maybe if we watch long enough to understand, we can get some answers and figure out why we're here or where here is."

Kinder shook his head. He backed away from her and bumped into the dining room table. Immediately, his ears were filled with screams. A woman was gasping, turning green, and grabbing at her throat, clawing at her face. She couldn't breathe. He watched as she fell face-first into a bowl of soup that spilled over the sides to wet her sandy blonde hair. Then he gasped and yanked his hand away. "The screamer was angry that time," he said. "He poisoned someone. I don't like this, and I want to go home."

Flower walked over to him. She took his hand tenderly, but he winced like she'd slapped him. Maybe he was expecting to see more visions. Maybe just the sense of touch had become trauma now. Flower frowned and looked him in the eye. "We don't know where home is or how to get there, Kin. What else are we going to do? Go back out there and wander through the green nothingness and hope we magically make it back home? This could help."

Kinder frowned, but he knew she was right. He nodded. "Okay, but I don't want to touch the table again."

"Okay."

"So what do we start with?"

"You pick."

He thought for a moment. He didn't know what to pick. He hated all of it and the whole idea. Finally, he said, "Why don't we both just go sit on the couch? That seems the easiest."

Flower gave him a reassuring smile, took his hand, and led the way.

House of Abandoned Things

Coming soon

THE DEATH DIGGER

BOE HEALY

WITH CHISTO HEALY

About the Author

Boe is the author of the Death Digger and has many more books in the works and on the way. It's all up to Daddy to type them up and make them sound better until he's old enough to do that part himself. All his stories take place in the same universe and are somehow connected. Kinder and Flower appear in a story in the upcoming charity anthology Strength Within and the upcoming book House of Abandoned Things. The Wizard of the Woods is in that books and also Boe's upcoming book, The Cursed Baby. He has stories that dad embellished a bit too much and he's not allowed to read in Body Horror Volume 2 by Baynam Books press and Splatology Volume 2. They are still connected to his universe. There are only four people in his world that have magic, the Witch of the World in the Death Digger, The Wizard of the Woods, The Warlock of the Water and the Sorcerer of Shadows. The Sorcerer is in his Splatology story, "Guts" and the Warlock is yet to be featured but will. His Body Horror story is about a woman who falsely believes she has magic and the consequences of that. He has another short story in the upcoming anthology Tales from the Hearth that features the Wizard of the Wood and the Sorcerer of Shadows and further expands the universe referencing the Guts story in Splatology 2 and this book.

Boe is an amazing little guy. He loves his friends, his parents, siblings, and grandparents, and his pets. He also loves scary, spooky things but doesn't like jump scares. He wants to own all of the animatronics. He loves drawing and zombies and wishes all his favorite prank shows were not cancelled. He isn't on social media yet so you have to talk to his dad, Chisto Healy.

Boe does love letters and correspondence though and people who love his books. He saw a TikTok review of the Death Digger and was so happy that he painted a heart, signed it, and mailed it to the reviewer. He has big plans and dreams of movies of his stories as well as toy lines and maybe even a Spirit Halloween animatronic....fingers crossed. He wants David Howard Thornton to play Truman Woodking in the movie or, and I quote..."It would be so funny if the Wood King was Jason Momoa in a Jason Momoa mask. Like what the what??? Haha ha. You should ask him." Unfortunately, I don't know Jason Momoa. If you do, let him know that Boe has a question.

THE END FOR NOW

Find out what happens to Kinder and Flower next in the
upcoming...

House of Abandoned Things
By Boe Healy